This is my o...

Through the sw... ...w him. A man dr... ...to toe—camouflaged in the storm. Though he was skiing uphill against the pelting wind, he moved with great speed, driving his long skis forward. His technique amazed her.

"Who are you?" Shana asked once he'd approached.

"Sergeant Luke Rawlins."

A soldier? Though she was dizzy and weak, she cracked a smile. It seemed that the cavalry had skied over the hill and come to her rescue. All she could see of his face was a firm, stubborn jaw.

With a huge effort, she stood upright, knee-deep in snow. Her legs felt like rubber. The cold had drained the last bit of strength from her muscles.

Before she could tell him that she was fine, her eyelids closed. She was falling through the swirling snow into unconsciousness.

CASSIE MILES

FOOTPRINTS IN THE SNOW

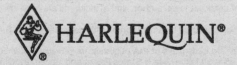

HARLEQUIN®

TORONTO • NEW YORK • LONDON
AMSTERDAM • PARIS • SYDNEY • HAMBURG
STOCKHOLM • ATHENS • TOKYO • MILAN • MADRID
PRAGUE • WARSAW • BUDAPEST • AUCKLAND

To the brave men and women of the
10th Mountain Division. And, as always, to my
favorite Marine sergeant, Rick Hanson.

ISBN-13: 978-0-373-88722-5
ISBN-10:   0-373-88722-1

FOOTPRINTS IN THE SNOW

ABOUT THE AUTHOR

Cassie Miles lives in a Denver high-rise with a view of the Front Range through her office window—a huge temptation to get outside and play. After a broken ankle a few years ago, she hung up her skis, but still enjoys hiking, climbing and sitting in a grove of aspen, reading a book.

Books by Cassie Miles

HARLEQUIN INTRIGUE

694—THE SECRET SHE KEEPS
769—RESTLESS SPIRIT
787—PROTECTING THE INNOCENT
820—ROCKY MOUNTAIN MYSTERY†
826—ROCKY MOUNTAIN MANHUNT†
832—ROCKY MOUNTAIN MANEUVERS†
874—WARRIOR SPIRIT
904—UNDERCOVER COLORADO‡
910—MURDER ON THE MOUNTAIN‡
948—FOOTPRINTS IN THE SNOW

†Colorado Crime Consultants
‡Rocky Mountain Safe House

CAST OF CHARACTERS

Shana Parisi—An exploration geologist on vacation in Colorado when she's swept up in a surprise blizzard.

Luke Rawlins—A sergeant in the 10th Mountain Division who has already seen action on the front lines.

Enrico Fermi—Nobel Prize–winning physicist who worked on the Manhattan Project.

Dr. Douglas & Dr. Schultz—Coworkers with Dr. Fermi.

Verne Hughes—Captain in charge of operations at Camp Hale.

Henry Harrison—Private First Class, conscripted into the 10th.

Edward Martin—Private First Class in the 10th.

Jack Swenson—Expert ski instructor and mountain man from Aspen.

Chapter One

Shana Parisi knew better than to leave the well-marked cross-country ski trail in the mountains outside Leadville. Above all, she believed in following the rules. Her logical, predictable nature served her well in her work as an exploration geologist for AMVOX Oil.

But today was somehow different. Acting on impulse, she'd stepped off the marked trail and gone exploring. Ignoring the beginning twinges of a headache, she'd skied from one interesting geological feature to another. These mineral-rich mountains were like a trip to Disneyland, especially since she'd spent the past year and a half on assignment in Kuwait. Colorado felt so clean, so fresh, so incredibly all-American.

She poked around the edges of an open pit mine. Studied the striation on a granite cliff. And entered a natural cave pocked with dark crystals, several of which found their way into her pocket along with an unusual shard of glassy green that looked like trinite.

Outside the cave, she slipped her boots into the bindings of her short backcountry skis, fastened the tethers and inhaled a gasp of the thin mountain air. Her lungs burned. Glancing at her wristwatch, she saw that she'd been out here for over three hours. Too long. Her slight headache had turned into a real killer.

Adjusting her goggles, she peered downhill at a wide slope bordered by thick pine forest on either side and tried to remember where she'd left the cross-country trail. Downhill to the left. Or to the right? Every year dozens of people got lost in these mountains. Some were never found.

Surely, she hadn't gone too far off track. Reaching up, she tightened the scrunchie that held her thick black hair up in a ponytail. Earlier, she'd taken off her heavy gloves and parka; the May weather was warm enough for skiing in just a down vest and turtleneck.

It was colder now. Heavy gray clouds roiled overhead, and darker clouds were coming in behind them. Snowflakes fell in nasty little sputters. Should she dig her warmer gear out of her backpack? Making that simple decision seemed difficult; the inside of her head was fuzzy. Something was wrong with her. Maybe altitude sickness. She was near the Continental Divide, over ten thousand feet. She needed to get off this mountain.

Though tempted to tuck into a ball and schuss downhill like an Alpine skier, she wasn't that skilled. Carefully, she traversed the ridge above the snow-covered slope. It took all of her concentration to coordinate thrusting with her skis and picking with her poles.

A fierce wind gusted around her, taking her breath away. A strange glow surrounded her—like a spotlight from the heavens. The wind became a deafening roar. Her body was weightless, disconnected. *What's happening?* She blinked slowly and everything returned to normal.

Then, the storm hit hard. An instant

blizzard. The heavens split open and dumped a truckload of snow on her head.

Her goggles smeared with moisture, and she could barely see. The freezing cold sank through her turtleneck and into her bones as she kept going. Though she was skiing furiously across the ridge, it felt as if she was standing still, suspended in the storm.

Turning to dig in with her edges, her skis stuttered across a patch of ice then slipped out from under her. A scream wrenched from her throat as she went flying. Her boots broke free from the bindings, and she released the poles. In a somersault, she landed on her backpack and slid downhill. Her skis, still attached by tethers, crashed beside her. She dug in the heels of her boots, fighting until finally she came to a stop.

When she struggled to stand, her feet sank deep into the snowpack, and she sprawled backward. With her heart beating rapidly, she couldn't catch her breath. She was dizzy, light-headed. The entire world was shrouded in white. And cold. God, it was cold.

Forcing herself up, she lurched and stumbled again, falling forward on her hands and knees. A wave of nausea surged in her belly. She vomited into the snow.

She needed to pull herself together, but she couldn't move. Did she hit her head when she fell? Was she paralyzed? More likely, she was in early stage hypothermia. A seductive lassitude. *This is what happens when you break the rules.*

It occurred to her that she might die. Alone. Unmarried and without children. There would be no one to mourn her passing except for her globe-trotting diplomat father whose greatest concern would be to choose the most appropriate coffin.

She lay back in the snow, too cold to care what happened to her. The roaring winds swept over her. In their wake came confusion. And then, a strong sense of certainty. She was meant to be here at this place and in this time. *This is my destiny.*

Through the swirling eddies of snow, she saw him. A man dressed in white from head to toe—camouflaged in the storm. Though he was skiing uphill against the pelting wind, he moved with great speed, driving his long skis forward. His technique amazed her. This guy was an incredible Nordic skier. A real athlete.

By the time she forced herself to sit up, he was beside her. She peered up at him. "Who are you?"

"Sergeant Luke Rawlins, 10th Mountain Division."

A soldier? Though she was dizzy and weak, she cracked a smile. It seemed that the cavalry had skied over the hill and come to her rescue. His head was covered by the white hood of his fur-lined parka. His eyes were hidden behind goggles. All she could see of his face was a firm, stubborn jaw.

With a huge effort, she stood upright, knee-deep in snow. Her legs felt like rubber. The cold had drained the last bit of strength from her muscles.

Before she could tell him that she was fine, her eyelids closed. She was falling through the whirling snow into unconsciousness.

IN HIS ONE-ROOM CABIN, Luke pulled the wet turtleneck up and over her head. She wasn't wearing a bra. Though his purpose in stripping off her wet clothes was to get her dried off and warmed up, he couldn't help looking. Her body was slim, but she curved in all the right places. The flare from her slender waist to her hips was sheer perfection. Her olive skin was smooth and unblemished except for three little moles that formed a triangle above her hip bone. Her breasts were small but exquisite—more beautiful than the marble statues he'd seen in Italy.

It had been a long time since he'd been with a naked woman. Nearly half a year. Before he shipped out for the front lines. Before he'd been wounded.

The woman he held in his arms groaned. Her head lifted for a moment before lolling forward. He tugged one of his army-issued T-shirts over her head and shoulders, then stretched her out on the bed and pulled up the covers to her chin.

Sitting beside her on the edge of the bed, he held her wrist to check her pulse. The beat was steady and stable; she was going to be all right after she warmed up. Though she'd taken one hell of a fall, she had no broken bones. Tomorrow, she'd feel the bruises.

Her nose wiggled as she stirred in her sleep. Then she sighed and went quiet again. She was beautiful, a regular sleeping beauty. Her thick black hair framed her face. Delicate eyebrows arched above her full lashes. Her best feature was her full, pouty lips. She had the kind of mouth that begged to be kissed.

When he'd rescued her from the blizzard, she'd looked like hell with snow matting her hair, her complexion drained and her lips tinged with blue. What had she been doing out here? This wasn't a sanctioned area; she shouldn't have been up here, but he was glad she'd broken the rules. This pretty lady— whoever she was—made a good diversion.

Only a few hours ago, Luke had received his orders to return to the front lines of battle. In less than a week, he'd be shipped back to hell. He wasn't a coward, but the order scared him. He remembered too well. Too many scenes of carnage were burned in his memory. When he closed his eyes, he saw the blood and the devastation. Buildings shattered. People torn apart. His ears still echoed with the cries of dying men and women. He felt the pain of his own wounds and relived the moment when he had been shot, when he saw his own death and welcomed it.

He didn't want to go back. Except for one thing.

He glanced toward the snapshot on the table. A picture of an eight-year-old boy with thick, curly black hair. His skinny chest thrust proudly as he waved to the camera. *Roberto.* Though Luke needed no reminder of the boy, he always carried that photo with him. He'd made a promise to Roberto. *I'll come back for you.* That solemn vow was more important to him than the war or his dedication to the 10th Mountain Division or even his own survival. Roberto was the reason Luke would return to the front. Though it seemed impossible to find one small boy among the multitude of orphans left by the war, he had to try.

When Luke came to the cabin tonight, he'd been hoping to find his sense of purpose. Because he was going to need every bit of his strength and courage to find Roberto and make everything turn out okay, he needed a reason to believe in himself again. And the storm had brought this strange woman to him.

He hadn't noticed her on the slope until he heard a yelp and saw her crashing out of control. She'd been a long way uphill from where he'd been standing, and he had to backtrack and circle around before he could reach her. She was damned lucky that he'd shown up when he did.

He'd saved her life. The odds against him being nearby at the exact moment when she crashed were a million to one. And if he hadn't been here, she would have frozen to death in this freak spring blizzard. Lucky for her. And for him, too.

The fact that he'd been there—at the right place and in the right time to save her—gave him satisfaction. It was almost enough to renew his spirit, almost enough to make him believe in the possibility of redemption.

Leaving her bedside, he went to the table and poured a double shot of Jack Daniel's into a mug. Holding the cup aloft, he toasted her. "Here's looking at you."

She groaned. Her eyelids fluttered.

Luke savored his whiskey and waited patiently.

When she finally wakened, she bolted upright to a sitting posture. Her dark brown eyes were huge and luminous. "Where am I?"

"One of the mountain huts constructed by the 10th Mountain Division."

Though she nodded in apparent understanding, he saw confusion in her rapidly darting gaze. Her lips worked before forming words. "I've always wanted to stay in one of these huts. It's almost impossible to get a reservation."

Though her words didn't make sense—a reservation?—she was relatively coherent. He nodded toward a cup of water on a chair beside the bed. "You should drink something."

"Right. I'm probably dehydrated."

As she sipped the water, his gaze went again to those full, ripe lips. His temperature rose. The memory of her lush naked body lingered in his mind.

He reached for the opened pack of Lucky Strike cigarettes on the table. "Smoke?"

"I quit, but I don't mind if you do. You're Luke. Is that right?"

He nodded. "And you are?"

"Shana Parisi."

"Nice to meet you, Shana Parisi." He liked the way her name rolled off his tongue. "How are you feeling?"

"Fine, except for the headache from hell."

"I assessed your physical condition. Your vitals are strong. I got you warmed up before you went into hypothermia, but you probably have altitude sickness. I'm guessing you haven't been at this elevation for more than a day or two."

"Your guess is correct."

"Where are you from?"

"Most recently, Kuwait. Before that, Thailand."

He hadn't expected that response. Kuwait? Thailand? She was turning into a very interesting diversion. "What brings you to Colorado?"

With a frown, she rubbed at her temple. "I'm a geologist. I work for AMVOX Oil, and we're looking into an oil shale operation on the western slope."

A geologist. That explained the rock

samples he'd found in her pockets. Luke finished off the dregs of his Jack Daniel's, glad for the whiskey warmth that spread through him and lightened his mood. He sure as hell hadn't expected to be smiling tonight.

She eyed him curiously. "You knew exactly what was wrong with me. Are you a doctor?"

"Trained as a medic," he said. "But it wasn't a complicated diagnosis to figure out that somebody who was turning into a human Popsicle might be going into hypothermia."

"When does the headache go away?"

"After a couple of aspirin. First, you need to eat something to elevate your blood sugar."

He crossed the two steps from the table to the bed and held out a Baby Ruth. When she took it from him, their hands touched. An electric spark shot up his arm.

She'd felt it, too. A gasp escaped her lips. Her dark brown eyes widened in surprise.

"Thank you," she whispered. "For the chocolate."

Shana couldn't quite believe the explosion

of energy **and** awareness that came when they accidentally touched. That electric sensation was almost enough to make her forget that her head ached and her body was stiff and sore. Luke Rawlins was quite a man.

Immediately she knew that she needed to be careful around him. He reminded her of a lot of the guys she'd worked with on exploration and drilling sites. They fancied themselves to be superstuds, and she'd learned long ago to keep her distance. She didn't want to be just another notch on the bedpost.

Purposefully, she looked away from Luke and concentrated on the tangible facts. She was glad to be here and to be warm, blessedly warm. A cast-iron potbellied stove stood near the door where their parkas hung on hooks. There were no extra frills in this small, one-room cabin lit by the amber glow of lanterns. A hut. She knew a bit about this system of simple log cabins that had been constructed in the 1940s by the 10th Mountain Division. In Leadville, there were dozens of memorials to these World War II heroes. "Didn't you say that you were with the 10th Mountain Division?"

"That's right."

"Those guys were supposed to be the best skiers, mountain climbers and sharpshooters in the world. Elite commandos."

"We still are."

As she peeled the wrapper off her Baby Ruth, she dared to study this soldier in his army-green fatigues—kind of a weird outfit for somebody who was on vacation at a mountain hut. But she was willing to excuse this minor eccentricity. The man had saved her life. Also, he was remarkably good-looking with deep-set blue eyes and the tanned complexion of an outdoorsman. His brown hair was short in a no-nonsense military cut that worked for him. She guessed that he was in his early thirties. If she'd been in the market for a man, he'd be the right age.

But she wasn't looking. Or was she? There was a sense of destiny about being here, being with him. *Destiny? Yeah, sure.* She believed in science, not kismet. Trying to ignore the twinges of pain inside her head, she nibbled at her candy bar and sipped the water. Rehydration was important.

He tapped a cigarette from the pack,

flipped open a Zippo lighter and lit up. Though she hated the tobacco smell, she was pleased. The fact that he had at least one disgusting habit was proof that he wasn't perfect. *Not the right guy for me.*

When he stood, she realized how tall he was—at least four inches over six feet. His body was lean but muscular with square shoulders, and he was obviously in excellent condition. Even in his poorly fitted fatigues, his muscular thighs bulged.

"I should thank you again," she said. "You saved my life."

"My pleasure." He went to the potbellied stove, opened the latched door and laid another piece of wood on the fire.

His pleasure? A shiver of awareness rippled through her. Beneath the quilts and blankets on the bed, she wore nothing but an oversize olive-drab T-shirt. Near the door, she saw her ski pants and her turtleneck hung up to dry. But she didn't remember getting undressed. Her fingers plucked at the cotton fabric of T-shirt. "Is this yours?"

"I had to strip off those wet clothes so you

could warm up. But don't worry. I kept my eyes closed."

Stripped naked by a stranger. She should have been humiliated, wildly embarrassed. Kept his eyes closed? *Yeah, right.*

When she gazed accusingly into his coolly assessing blue eyes, she saw a hint of approval. Then he grinned. Apparently, he'd been pleased by what he'd seen when he changed her clothes.

In normal circumstances, she would have lashed out, making it very clear that he would never ever see her naked again. Instead, a lovely warmth blossomed inside her. She could do a lot worse than being swept off her feet by Luke Rawlins. "I'll have that aspirin now."

He tossed her a small glass bottle and returned to the chair where he sat and stretched out his long legs. Leaning back, he took a puff on his cigarette and exhaled a cloud of blue smoke.

Slightly mesmerized, she watched. He even made smoking look sexy. Quickly, she gulped down three aspirin. She really ought to get out of here before she did something she'd regret. Like throwing herself into his arms. Or ripping off her T-shirt. Or, better yet, tearing off his clothes piece by piece. "I should go now. I've already imposed too much on your hospitality."

"It's late, Shana. Almost dark. You're going nowhere tonight."

She peered through the frost-rimed glass of the only window in the cabin. Outside, it was heavy and gray but the blizzard seemed to have stopped. She was aware of the wind whistling through the branches of the pine trees and sweeping against the log walls of the cabin. "Do you have a car? Or a snow-mobile? Some kind of transportation?"

"Just my skis."

"Maybe I could call for help. Do you have my pack?"

He went toward the door, picked up her pack and set it on the bed beside her. She sifted through the contents until she found her cell phone, which was totally dead. "Broken. I must have landed on it when I fell."

She was stranded. Tucked away in a cozy, warm cabin with the sexiest man she'd ever seen. This felt like a fantasy. A dream. But he was here and real—far too potent to vanish when she blinked her eyes.

Needing to assess the situation, she threw off the blankets and climbed out of the bed. In a few strides, she crossed to the door and pulled it open. A blast of cold hit her bare legs. Though the snow had stopped, a drift came all the way up to the cabin's door and trickled inside. They were in the forest at the edge of a clearing. She saw no sign of other houses. No lights. No roads. Nothing but complete isolation.

Luke came up behind her and shoved the door closed. "You're here for the night."

When she looked up into his face, she didn't want to leave. Wearing only his T-shirt, she should have been cold. Instead, a glowing heat churned through her veins. Strange. She was light-headed, oddly disconnected.

He touched her forehead. "You're hot."

"So are you," she said. "If we rub together, maybe we'll start a forest fire."

A smile lifted the corner of his mouth. "I meant to say that you might have a fever."

"But I don't feel sick. Not really sick." But

not herself. Her common sense seemed to have vanished, whisked away by the swirling snows on the mountain. She'd been transported to a magical place where normal concerns and hesitations did not apply.

Reaching out, she placed her palm flat against his chest. Through his army fatigues, she felt the steady, strong beating of his heart. The rhythm echoed through her and synchronized perfectly with her own pulse—two hearts beating as one. She was a part of him. Inseparable and needing a deeper connection.

She tilted her chin up. Her lips parted.

When he kissed her, he took his time. She tasted whiskey on his mouth. Slowly, he deepened the kiss.

His arms surrounded her, supporting her. His body pressed against hers. She seemed to rise off the floor, floating on a cloud. A spiral of tingling sensation unfurled and spread from her head to her heart to every intimate part of her.

When his lips left hers, she gazed up at his ruggedly handsome face. Her vision went hazy. Her headache became a steady pulse. Throbbing, but not painful.

She couldn't believe this was really happening. A strong, gorgeous man had appeared from nowhere to sweep her into his arms and rescue her from certain death. He was her knight in shining ski gear.

Though she barely had the strength to stand, she knew his strong arms would never let her fall. Dazed and in shock, she abandoned herself to this swirling fantasy.

Chapter Two

Shana stumbled off balance. Her back rested against the cabin wall. The cold from outside crept through the logs and chilled her spine, contrasting the fire that burned inside her—an intense heat generated by his kiss.

"Shana," he whispered, "are you all right?"

She wanted to say yes, but her head was spinning and her knees were weak. "I need to sit down."

He guided her the few paces to the narrow bed and helped tuck her bare legs under the covers.

Stretched out on the bed, she looked up at him. So handsome. So gentle. This man had saved her life. He was her real-live hero, and he kissed like an expert.

She wanted more kisses, a lot more. This

was crazy. Making love to a total stranger? Shana knew better. Years of working in the field, mostly with men, had taught her self-control. But she wasn't at a job site. This cabin, tucked away in the mountains, was a different reality. Regular rules and restrictions did not apply.

When he started to rise from the bed, she sat up and caught hold of his arm. "Don't go."

He cocked an eyebrow. "Do you need something?"

You. I need you. She wanted him to stay close beside her, to kiss her again.

"This doesn't seem fair," she said. "I'm nearly naked, and you're wearing all those clothes."

She raised her arm and stroked the bristly stubble on his jaw. With a fingertip, she traced a line from his mouth to his chin and down his throat. Aware that her behavior was utterly inappropriate, she began to unbutton his shirt. The effort took all her concentration. Her fingers lacked dexterity.

"Shana, I don't think this is—"

"Don't think." Never before had she been

so bold. She must be delirious. "I want this shirt off."

"Let me."

He unfastened the buttons and slipped off his shirt, then he pulled his T-shirt over his head. His arms and shoulders were lean yet muscular. A sprinkle of dark hair coated his chest. Below his collarbone, she saw a ragged scar. The suturing had been rushed, clumsy. Another scar crossed his rib cage.

She ran her thumb across the mark on his chest. "What happened?"

"The war happened."

He'd been injured in battle. He really was a hero. That fact jolted her back toward reality, reminding her that there was a real world outside this cabin. "I'm sorry, Luke."

"Don't cry for me. I survived."

He wasn't being macho. Just stating a fact.

She held the dog tags that hung around his neck. "Name, rank and serial number," she said. "Blood type O negative. You're a universal donor."

"That's right."

"What does the *P* stand for?"

"Protestant."

"Or maybe," she said, "the *P* stands for *Perfect*."

"If you knew me better, you wouldn't say that."

"What's your fatal flaw?"

"Right now? I'm thinking how good it would be to make love to you."

She nodded, and her brain rattled painfully. She winced. Though she desperately wanted to stay alert, her eyelids drooped. "Making love," she murmured. "Not a problem."

"You need to rest. You're already half-unconscious. I won't take advantage of you."

"Rest." That sounded good. "Sleep."

He leaned her back, laid her down on the pillow. Though she still had the urge to make love, her body was limp. So tired.

As she closed her eyes, she felt Luke lightly kiss her forehead. He was moving away from her. Yet, in her mind, she could feel his strong arms wrapped tightly around her. The heat of his body permeated her flesh.

She might be dreaming, but this was the most realistic fantasy she'd ever had. She could smell him. Her nostrils flared. A musky scent.

Their clothing melted away, and she experienced the amazing moment when their naked bodies met. The hair on his chest rubbed against her breasts, and her nipples tightened. She groaned with anticipation.

If she opened her eyes, she was certain to see his smile. His firm, stubborn jaw. The shining, intoxicating blue of his eyes.

She was ready for him. Her legs parted, welcoming him. Needing him. She never wanted to wake up. Being with Luke was the right thing. The only thing. She had to have this man. This snow-driven, crystalline fantasy was her destiny.

THE NEXT MORNING, sunlight poured through the window of the small cabin and slanted across the blankets that covered Shana on the narrow bed. Her body ached from injuries she suffered when she crashed down the slope, but she wasn't complaining. Last night had been fantastic, even if it was only a dream. She lay very still, not really wanting to face the reality of a new day.

Slowly, she opened her eyelids and saw Luke, fully dressed and tending to the fire in the potbellied stove. Though he was the same handsome man who had rescued her, she sensed that today was far different from yesterday and last night. Also, her headache had returned.

"Aspirin," she croaked.

At the sound of her voice, he turned toward her. His smile was polite but wary. "Aspirin and water are on the chair beside the bed."

She wasn't exactly sure what she expected him to say, but that wasn't it. Vaguely irritated, she reached for the mug, downed three aspirin and lay back on the pillows. Beneath the sheets she was naked and terribly aware of her vulnerability.

"Are you hungry?" he asked.

Last night, she'd been starving...but not for food. She craved him. Of course, that wasn't what he was talking about. "I could eat something."

"My supplies are sparse." He reached up to a high shelf and grabbed an opened cardboard box that he placed on the table. "I've got a couple of K rations I swiped from the quartermaster."

"K rations?"

"Survival food to carry in combat. If the enemy doesn't kill you, this stuff will."

"You're talking about an MRE, meal ready to eat. When I was in Kuwait, some of the soldiers had them."

When he placed the box on the bed in front of her, she wrinkled her nose in disgust. The prepackaged energy food had all the appeal of eating tree bark, but she needed to build her strength if she hoped to ski back to civilization. After peeling off the wrapper, she forced herself to bite into the square chunk of tasteless calories. It crumbled in her mouth like sand.

"How about coffee?" Luke asked.

"Oh, yes."

He went to the potbellied stove. Using a dish towel, he lifted a metal pot from the burner and poured steaming liquid into a mug that looked like vintage Fiestaware. A quaint touch, she thought. These mountain huts had been built in the 1940s and the crockery matched that era. So did the furniture. The Formica table with aluminum legs and matching chairs looked almost new thanks to the retro craze.

When he handed her the mug, there was no spark of electricity. No special thrill. They were strangers again. *So that's the way it's going to be. Well, fine.*

With a dispassionate gaze, she studied him. Still gorgeous, but there was something odd about the way he was dressed. His fatigues were the old-fashioned army drab instead of the usual beige or green camouflage. The fabric seemed stiff and heavy. "You mentioned that you were in the army."

"Stationed at Camp Hale. Or Camp Hell, as we like to call it."

"From the 10th Mountain Division."

He pointed to the crossed sword insignia on the sleeve of his white parka, which hung from a peg near the door. "We climb to conquer."

Shana took a sip of the bitter coffee, which was nothing like the thick, rich espresso she'd grown to adore while in Kuwait. "Tell me about Camp Hale."

"Construction started in 1942 under Charles Minnie Dole who started the 10th to train for cold weather warfare. At the high point, there were ten thousand men stationed here. Now, most everybody has shipped out."

She was no World War II buff, but Shana was certain that Camp Hale no longer existed. In the hotel where she was staying in Leadville, there were several black-and-white photos of the historic Camp Hale site and the famous troops who had fought bravely in Europe at the end of the war. A long time ago. "What are you doing here?"

"Me and a skeleton crew pulled guard duty for a government project." He checked his wristwatch. "I need to report back real soon."

"You're leaving me here?"

"The rest will do you good," he said. "I'll come back this afternoon and help you get into town."

She tasted disappointment with her coffee. Last night, he'd been clear about making no promises that they'd be together. But she expected more from him. Something. Anything.

She glanced toward the cabin door. Her short metallic skis were propped against the wall beside his long wood skis. Hickory skis with old-fashioned cable bindings? The laminated wood shafts of his ski poles were equally antiquated with a twisted bamboo basket.

A rifle also stood near the door. "What kind of gun is that?"

"A .30 caliber Garand with an eight round clip. Standard issue."

"Not really." In the Middle East, she'd become familiar with the weaponry used by U.S. troops. "What about the M16? Or the M4 Carbine? The .50 caliber sniper rifle?"

"A .50 caliber?" He scoffed. "There's no such thing."

"Every soldier in Iraq carries at least one of those weapons."

"Iraq?" His eyebrows lifted. "Yeah, I remember now. You were in Kuwait. The Middle East."

"I know a little bit about military equipment."

"So you're an expert."

"I didn't say that." Why was he so cranky? "I was just noticing that you have some old-fashioned equipment. Like those wood skis."

He fired a glare in her direction but said

nothing. If she'd been smart, Shana would have followed his example and kept her mouth shut, but she continued, "I didn't even know they made bindings like that anymore."

"Now you're an expert on ski equipment." He looked down at her from his towering height. "I should have guessed from your skill on the slopes when you slid halfway down the mountain on your butt."

"That wasn't my fault. How could I know a blizzard was coming?"

"A sky full of snow clouds should have been a clue."

"I get your point." She adjusted the blankets around her. "I wasn't being careful. Maybe because of the altitude sickness."

"Maybe," he conceded.

"I'm usually a rational, logical person." At her new assignment in Rifle, she'd be the project manager. "I'm very responsible."

When she stared directly into his intense blue eyes, she saw a brief spark. A flicker of memory from last night?

"I guess," he drawled, "I'll have to take your word about being responsible."

While she groped in her mind for a snappy

comeback, he pulled his snow pants over his fatigues and sat on the chair to lace up his boots, which were also old-fashioned in design. She tried to imagine why Luke— who was obviously an experienced skier— would be using such antiquated equipment.

"I know," she said. "You're doing some kind of historical reenactment. Something about the early days of the 10th Mountain Division. Am I right?"

"I don't have time to play games, and the 10th isn't history." He frowned. "Are you feeling okay? You sound a little Looney Tunes this morning."

"I'm fine," she snapped. "As soon as possible, I'm out of here."

"Whatever you say."

Wrong! He was supposed to tell her that he'd enjoyed their kiss last night. At the very least, he should offer a couple of light compliments. "I know you enjoyed it. Last night was every man's fantasy. Being trapped in a cabin with a naked woman."

"Depends on the woman," he said.

"Are you telling me I'm not your type?" If she hadn't still been nearly naked, she would have leaped from the bed and smacked him. "I suppose you prefer brainless blondes."

"Not really. I wouldn't kick Betty Grable out of the sack, but Rita Hayworth is my pinup. You'd look a little bit like her if you'd—"

"Stop it," she snapped. "Rita Hayworth. Camp Hale. Wood skis. Exactly what year do you think it is?"

He slipped on his parka, grabbed his skis and opened the cabin door. "It's 1945."

Her jaw dropped. "What?"

"I'll be back this afternoon. Rest easy, Shana."

The door closed firmly behind him.

This was just typical of her luck. She finally let down her guard and allowed herself to experience the fantasy of the moment, and the guy was certifiably insane.

She pushed aside the K rations. That was another 1945 term—K ration instead of MRE. Did he really believe it was over sixty years ago?

Did it matter if he did? His message was pretty darn clear. He was done with her. *Well, fine.* She was done with him, too. No way was she going to wait around in this dinky little cabin for him to come back. Shana could find her own way back to the ski trails and the parking lot where she'd left her rental car.

When she crawled out of the bed, it felt as if every muscle in her body had been strained. A gigantic purple bruise decorated her thigh. She stretched and took a couple of cleansing breaths, hoping to move beyond the pain.

While she dressed, she forced down another cup of coffee, more water and another few bites of the disgusting K ration food substitute. What a lousy way to start her time in Colorado!

Even though Luke had been utterly obnoxious, she probably ought to leave him a note, explaining that she'd decided not to stick around. As she poked around on the table looking for a paper and pencil, she found a black-and-white photograph of a young kid with curly hair. Luke's son? On the back of the picture was a note written in fountain pen. "Roberto. Christmas, 1944."

The edges of the photo were frayed, indicating that it had been handled a lot. Carefully, Shana returned the picture to the table.

In her pack, she found a confirmation for her hotel room and scribbled a note on the back.

Thanks for saving my life. Going to town. Goodbye forever, Shana.

Before leaving, she glanced around the cabin. So much for windswept fantasies. It was time to get back to the real world. She grabbed her skis and trudged out the door.

As if to compensate for her dark mood, the weather was spectacular. Brilliant sunlight illuminated clear blue skies and sparkled like diamonds on the new-fallen snow that decorated the pine trees surrounding the forest. Yesterday's blizzard was already beginning to melt.

She shoved her boots into the bindings and fastened the tethers. Her first gliding step was agony. When she got back to the hotel in Leadville, Shana intended to spend the rest of the day soaking in the tub, healing her physical wounds.

She followed the tracks of Luke's skis through the forest. The more she moved, the more her muscles loosened up. Except for the bruise on her hip and the remnant of a headache, she was okay. Slowly, she made her way through the forest to an open slope that seemed familiar. Was this where she'd fallen yesterday?

Though she wasn't sure which direction led back to the marked cross-country ski trails, she figured that if she kept heading downhill, she'd eventually find her way. She'd barely eased the tip of her ski onto the slope when she heard a gunshot.

Startled, she pulled back and hid in the trees. Why would anybody be shooting up here? It wasn't hunting season. She thought of Luke and his rifle. He'd claimed to be doing guard duty on a government project. War games? Glancing back over her shoulder, she thought of returning to the cabin and barring the door. Then she saw them.

About twenty yards downhill, two men dressed in black skied across the slope, moving fast and ducking down. One of them turned and fired wildly with a handgun.

Shana ducked. This was crazy. His bullet could have gone anywhere.

Luke appeared. Clad in his all-white parka and ski pants, he was camouflaged against the glittering white snow, but nothing could hide his skill and dexterity on his long, wood skis. He moved fast, bursting out of the forest and onto the open slope. Halfway across, he swooshed to a halt, sending up a spray of powder snow. He dropped to one knee. With one smooth move, he flipped his Garand rifle from a sheath on his back into his gloved hands. Sighting down the barrel, he fired. Once. Then again.

One of the men Luke had been pursuing gave a pained shout. He was hit, but he didn't go down. He and his partner disappeared into the trees on the opposite side of the slope.

Luke set off in single-minded pursuit.

Shana couldn't believe what she was seeing, but she was dead certain that she wanted no part of this violence. What she needed was to get the hell away from here.

Desperately, she edged uphill, away from the fight. As she crested the slope, she found herself looking down into a wide valley. There were over a hundred rectangular barracks arranged in neat rows—housing for ten thousand men.

Smoke rose from some of the chimneys, and she saw a soldier leading a mule across the hard-packed snow. An old army jeep chugged on a snow-covered roadway in front of a large two-story house with two separate wings. There was a mess hall. Other administrative buildings. A barn.

This was Camp Hale. From 1945.

Chapter Three

This huge army base hadn't been here yesterday. It hadn't been here for the past fifty years. It didn't exist anymore.

Shana blinked furiously, hoping to erase the visual evidence. When she stared down the slope, nothing had changed. Camp Hale spread out before her like a black-and-white photograph come to life. Apparently, Luke wasn't crazy. *She was.*

Her mind searched for a logical explanation.

Possibly, the site had been recreated as a historical place. With all those barracks? Housing for ten thousand troops? The cost of running the base would be too high.

If someone had rebuilt Camp Hale, they had to have a lot of cash. A movie? That made more sense. Hollywood people might be extravagant enough to reconstruct the base to make a movie about the legendary 10th Mountain Division.

But when she peered down toward the camp, she saw nothing resembling the lights and cameras needed by a movie crew. Instead of a movie crew led by Steven Spielberg, there were soldiers in fatigues. The only vehicles were vintage army jeeps. And mules.

More gunfire echoed behind her, and she startled. The obvious escape led straight down the hill into the camp, but she didn't want to go there. Once she entered that 1945 world, she might never be able to return to her own time, her own millennium. She didn't want to be swallowed up by the past.

This vision had to be an illusion, an aftereffect of altitude sickness. Luke had told her it was 1945. His suggestion must have triggered this fantasy from the photographs she'd seen in Leadville.

A fantasy? That wasn't the way her mind worked. Shana was a scientist. Her life was based on rock-solid facts and rational analysis. She didn't believe in fairy tales and had very little need for imagination. Last night with Luke was the closest she'd ever come to a fantasy.

Did their kiss even happen? Or was that a part of this winter mirage? *Think, Shana.* Somehow this had to make sense. Maybe she'd died on the slopes and Camp Hale was limbo. She wasn't someone who…traveled backward through time.

This wasn't happening; she refused to accept Camp Hale no matter how real it looked. The important thing was to find her way back to reality. Forcing her legs to move, she turned away from the encampment. *Ignore it. Pretend that you never saw Camp Hale. Ski back to the rental car, back to Leadville.*

"Halt," came a shout from down the hill.

Two men—dressed like Luke in all-white snow gear—charged up the slope toward her. Their movements seemed labored; neither of them were as proficient on skis as Luke. While one man continued to approach, the other dropped to one knee and leveled a rifle at her chest.

"Raise your hands above your head."

Shana did as she was told. Even in an imaginary world, she had no desire to be shot.

"You're a girl," said the guy who reached her first. He turned and waved to his partner. "Lower your weapon."

He did as ordered and came toward them.

The first man asked, "What the hell are you doing up here, girlie?"

Though her mouth was dry, Shana forced words past her lips. "I'm with Luke. Luke Rawlins."

"No kidding?" He turned back to his partner again. "She says she's with Sergeant Rawlins."

The second man joined them. When he pushed back the fur-lined hood of his parka, she was surprised to see how young he looked. This tall, lanky kid couldn't have been more than eighteen. He frowned at her. "I don't believe it. The sergeant isn't a womanizer, and he knows better than to bring a girl up here."

"She could be a spy. Take a look at her skis. I've never seen anything like those before. They're made out of plastic."

"Fiberglass," Shana said. She'd spent enough time on drilling sites to know how to deal with men who didn't trust her opinions and skills. It was important to immediately establish that she wasn't a brainless twit. She kept her voice calm. "I'm sure there's an explanation for everything, gentlemen. May I lower my hands?"

"Not yet," said the young guy. He came close and patted her down in a clumsy frisk. "Take off that knapsack and hand it to me."

She obeyed his order and watched as the two of them pawed through the contents of her pack. The younger man flipped open her wallet. "International Driver's License," he said accusingly. "Your name is Shana Parisi?"

"Yes. And you are?"

"Private First Class Henry Harrison."

She turned to the other man. "And you?"

"I don't have to tell you my name."

He pushed back his hood, revealing black hair in a bowl cut like one of the Three Stooges. She decided to think of him as Moe. He took the wallet from Henry and studied her license. "Parisi, huh? Are you Italian?"

"My grandparents were from Italy. Naples."

"The land of Mussolini."

Moe and Henry exchanged a meaningful glance and nodded. The land of Mussolini? *Oh, please.* Anger surged through her veins. "I'm not a spy."

"Then what are you?" Moe demanded. "You're not one of those Mafiosos, are you? A girlfriend of Al Capone?"

Could he possibly be more stereotypical and insulting? Obviously, "political correctness" had not been part of the vocabulary in 1945. "Not all Italians are part of the Mafia."

Young Henry thrust her cell phone toward her. "What's this thing?"

"A telephone. It's not working right now."

"That's a load of malarkey." He gave a snort. "A telephone without wires. Like a walkie-talkie. This looks like spy equipment to me."

Moe snapped her wallet closed. "This license is a bad forgery. They got your birthday wrong. Says here that you were born in 1974. That's almost thirty years from now."

Because it's 1945. That idea was beginning to sink into her consciousness. These two men—Henry and Moe—were clearly from a bygone era.

"You got one more chance," Moe said, "And you better be telling me God's own truth. Why are you here in this restricted area?"

"If you talk to Luke," she said, "he can explain."

Moe scowled as he shoved her belongings into her backpack and tossed it toward her. "We'll take her to Luke," he said as if it was his very own idea. "Come on, Henry. Let's escort Miss Parisi into camp."

FRUSTRATION BOILED in Luke's blood. The men he'd been chasing had gotten away clean. He'd failed in his pursuit.

When he'd spotted them, they were peering down at Camp Hale with binoculars. They fled when he approached, then opened fire with their handguns. Luke was sure he'd winged one of them before they skied out of range and hopped into a waiting vehicle. He should have had them, should have aimed more carefully, should have skied faster.

Though Captain Hughes hadn't reprimanded him, Luke knew he'd screwed up a simple mission of protecting the perimeters at Camp Hale. After his years of training in mountain combat, he should have been more effective.

And now, he had Shana to deal with.

He stormed into the vacant office where she was being held. Closing the door behind him, he said, "I told you to wait for me at the cabin."

"I don't take orders from you."

"Maybe you should. You're in serious trouble, lady."

As she stood and faced him, he realized that this was the first time he'd seen her fully dressed and in control. She was impressive, very composed. Her confidence was high, and her bearing reminded him of the lady officers in the Women's Army Auxiliary Corps.

With her thick black hair tamed in a knot at the nape of her neck and her maroon turtleneck tucked neatly into her black ski pants, she looked nothing like the passionate woman from last night...until she smiled with those full, ripe, kissable lips.

Calmly, she said, "I might have stayed in the cabin if you'd told me there were gunmen wandering the slopes. Or that I might be in danger."

"I didn't think you were."

"You should have explained."

She was right. He should have taken the time this morning to tell her that Camp Hale was heavily guarded while the scientists from Project Y were on the premises. Instead, he'd allowed his emotions to overrule his common sense.

When he woke up this morning and realized that he'd rescued such a beautiful woman, something inside him shifted. Their kiss reminded him that he was still alive, still capable of passion. Still a man.

He hadn't felt that way since his tour of duty in Italy when he saw the devastation of battle firsthand. Small villages shattered under the boot heel of war. Families torn asunder. The suffering. The pain.

Luke was a soldier; his duty was to follow orders. But the first time he'd looked into the eyes of a German soldier and pulled the trigger, the first time he saw a man die, he was changed. He'd gone numb inside. Become a hollow man.

Roberto had given him a reason to hope, but he had to leave the boy behind. The emptiness consumed him. He'd felt nothing until last night with Shana. This morning, he should have been thanking her instead of running away in confusion.

She cocked her head and looked up at him. "Why do your men think I'm a spy?"

"Are you?"

Her beautiful brown eyes narrowed to angry slits. "Of course not."

He shrugged. "If you were a spy, you wouldn't tell me."

Henry and Martin were convinced that she was Mata Hari. They'd waved her International Driver's License in front of his face, pointed to her weird fiberglass skis and the little mechanical device she claimed was a telephone. However, Henry and Martin were idiots. Luke didn't put much stock in their opinion.

He has suspicions of his own. Yesterday, she'd appeared out of nowhere. Last night, she attempted to seduce him. "You're pretty enough to be a spy."

"Give me a break." She scowled. "I work for AMVOX Oil. I'm a geologist. Remember?"

Though he didn't want to believe that she was spying, her profession dovetailed with the work of the government scientists he was here to protect. It would be a hell of a thing if she turned out to be the enemy. "We've had intruders in the vicinity. I don't suppose you were up here with anyone else."

"I saw you chasing two men. Shooting at them." She shook her head. "I have nothing to do with them."

Her beautiful dark eyes regarded him steadily and seriously. If she was lying, she was damn good at it. "I have to detain you, Shana. It's procedure. You'll have to stay here until we check out your background."

"That doesn't work for me. My project in Rifle starts in five days. I need to be there."

"This won't take long," he promised. "Just give me the name of someone I can call, someone who can verify that you're an innocent geologist on a ski trip."

"There isn't anyone I can call." Before his eyes, her composure crumbled. Her gaze dropped to the floor and stuck there. "I don't know anybody."

"Your supervisor," he suggested. "Or a family member."

"There's no one." She sank into the hard-backed chair beside the cleared desk, doubled over and buried her face in her hands. "I can't think."

The enormity of her situation weighed on her shoulders like a ten-ton boulder. How could she explain? Of course, Shana knew people, important people. Her father was a career diplomat with connections in high places. She knew the CEO for AMVOX. But none of those people were available. In 1945, her father would have been two years old.

She looked up at Luke. He leaned his hip against the wooden desk in this plain square office that was cleared of all paperwork. His arms folded across his chest. He'd been right when he said she was in serious trouble.

She was stranded here. Without a bank account. Neither her credit cards nor her ATM card would work. She was homeless, completely without resources.

"I don't have anyone I can contact." Not here. Not in 1945. "I can't remember…"

"Are you telling me that you have amnesia?"

She seized on this excuse. "That's right. I can't remember anything."

"Except that you were in the Middle East." His tone was suspicious. "You told me that last night."

What else had she said? Last night, they hadn't done much talking. Between her headache and her intense attraction to him, she hadn't told him much. Now, his lack of information might work to her advantage.

"I have amnesia." She rose to her feet to emphasize her words. "I need to get to a doctor in Leadville."

"We have medical personnel here on base."

But she didn't want to stay here, trapped in 1945. If she left Camp Hale, she might be able to find the way back to her own millennium. "I need a specialist, a psychiatrist. Or a neurologist. Please, Luke."

His jaw set in a firm, stubborn line that made her think he had little intention of accommodating her wishes. "Where were you staying in Leadville?"

"A hotel."

"Which hotel?"

Her lodging probably didn't have the same name as it did in 1945. It might not have even existed. "I don't remember the name. I left the receipt in your cabin. I wrote a goodbye note on the back."

"You must have driven to get up here. Where's your car parked?"

"When I was skiing, I got lost. I don't know where my car is." That much was true. "You have to take me to Leadville. From there, I can find my way back to Denver. Or I might find a specialist in Aspen."

"Aspen?" He gave her a puzzled look. "You won't find much of anything in that sleepy little town."

Of course not. The development of Aspen into a glittering, world-class ski resort took place after World War II. If she remembered correctly, returning soldiers from the 10th Mountain Division were largely responsible for that growth.

The door to the office swung open and a

stocky man dressed in old-fashioned ski knickers strode inside. "I have been looking for you, Luke. You promised to show me the best trails."

"Yes, sir."

"We will leave soon. Very soon." His accent was Italian. His dark eyes sparkled when he noticed Shana. "But first I must meet this charming young lady. You are?"

"Shana Parisi," she said. *"Buon giorno."*

Obviously delighted, he responded in Italian. Shana used rudimentary Italian she'd learned from her grandmother to make polite conversation about the weather and the scenery.

He took her hand and lifted it to his lips in a courtly gesture. "I am Enrico Fermi."

"The Nobel Prize winner?"

"You know my work?"

"Absolutely."

He was one of the most brilliant physicists of all time, the father of nuclear fission. She'd studied his theories, seen his face in textbooks. Fermi worked on the Manhattan project and had been at Los Alamos where the atom bomb was developed.

A realization struck her. The first atomic bomb test had taken place in 1945 at Alamogordo, New Mexico. Shana even recalled the date because it was the same as her sister's birthday, and their father always called her sister a bombshell. July 16, 1945.

"What's the date today?"

"May seventh," Luke said.

In two months, Dr. Enrico Fermi and the other scientists at Los Alamos would change the world.

Chapter Four

In the back of her mind, Shana heard the wail of a siren. An ambulance. Though faraway, the scream was all-consuming, echoing inside her skull.

She wanted to reach up and touch her head, but her arm wouldn't move. There were loud voices. Slamming doors.

Then a terrible silence.

IN THE OFFICE at Camp Hale, Shana glanced from Dr. Fermi to Luke. Had she heard an ambulance? How did she get here?

Coldly, Luke asked, "How do you know Dr. Fermi's work?"

Brushing aside her strange auditory hallucination, she tried to focus on an explanation. She reminded herself that this was

1945, and very few people were aware of the top secret Manhattan Project. No one—not even Fermi himself—had witnessed the mushroom-shaped cloud that would loom forever across political horizons. The bombing of Hiroshima and Nagasaki had not yet taken place.

The importance of those earthshaking events made her own predicament seem light as a Nerf ball. Still, she had to choose her words carefully. Or else she might find herself locked up in a prison, accused of treason. She avoided looking directly into Luke's honest blue eyes as she said, "Anyone who's studied physics knows Dr. Fermi. He won the Nobel." She turned to him. "Which year?"

"Nineteen thirty-eight," he said. "When I went to Sweden to collect my prize, I emigrated to the United States. Italy under the dictator, Mussolini, was unsafe for my family. My wife is Jewish."

"Our country is lucky to have you, sir." If Fermi had stayed in Europe, his work in nuclear fission might have led to another nation being the first to develop the atom bomb. "May I ask what you're doing at Camp Hale?"

"I am here with a team to explore some of the mining operations."

The logical deduction was that Fermi had come to Leadville to test the quality of uranium ore being mined in this area. A high grade of enriched uranium was needed to make yellow cake for the reactors.

"Perhaps I can help," she offered. "I'm a geologist."

"Bella e brillante," he said.

"Beautiful and smart?" she translated. "I don't know how true that is."

"No need for modesty." He tucked her arm through his. "Come. You will meet the rest of my team."

Luke cleared his throat. "I'm sorry, Dr. Fermi. Shana isn't feeling well. We were on our way to the infirmary."

"I feel much better," she said quickly. Fermi was offering her a way around Luke's difficult questions, and she'd be a fool not to take advantage. "I'd be delighted to meet the rest of Dr. Fermi's crew."

As they walked through the door, Luke leaned close and whispered, "I'm not letting you out of my sight. Not for one damn minute."

"Lucky you," she whispered back.

Shana knew her behavior was suspicious. If she actually had been a secret agent, her first order of business would be to get close to Dr. Fermi, to encourage him to trust her so she could kidnap him. But a far different agenda was taking form in her mind. There had to be a scientific explanation for how she'd traveled back in time. What could be better than to have one of the greatest theoretical physicists of all time helping her figure out the process? Unfortunately, she didn't think time travel and relativity were Fermi's specialty. "Do you know Dr. Einstein?" she asked.

"Albert? Sure, I do."

"What do you think of his theories of speed and time?"

Fermi gave an elaborate shrug, a gesture that reminded her of her Italian grandfather. "Until we are able to exceed the speed of light, his ideas will be untested. This is not to say they are untrue. Physics shows us that almost anything is possible."

"I like the way you think." Nothing was impossible. She'd shot backward in time.

Reversing the process ought to be within the realm of possibility.

"You are an interesting woman, Shana Parisi. *Bella e brillante.*"

She tossed a glance over her shoulder at Luke, who was positively fuming. His tense jaw made it look as if he was grinding his rear molars together. *Too bad!* If she had Dr. Fermi on her side, she didn't need Luke's approval.

They left the long whitewashed administrative building and stepped onto the sanded, hard-packed pathway that led through the snow. Dr. Fermi directed her toward the large two-story house where he and his crew were staying.

As they walked, two soldiers in full battle gear fell into step behind them. She assumed that their assignment was to protect Dr. Fermi, but they could also be keeping an eye on her because she was so terribly suspicious. The thought made her grin. Her personality had always been straightforward, direct and responsible. Hardly a woman of mystery.

In spite of the size of the camp and the

number of barracks, there were only a few soldiers on the pathway. She asked, "How many men are stationed here?"

"There are only a couple of administrative types and four rifle squads left. About sixty people altogether," Luke said. "Everybody else has shipped out to Italy. The Po Valley."

Dr. Fermi's fingers tightened on her arm. "The Apennine Mountains. In better days, it was a magnificent place for skiing and climbing."

"The war will be over soon," she promised. In May of 1945, it was almost a year since the D-day invasion. The Allied Forces were close to victory in Europe.

"Not soon enough." He turned to Luke. "In the meantime, we ski. Yes?"

"We will try to accommodate your request, sir."

"Tonight, I will commandeer the kitchen and make pasta for everybody. My wife's recipe is—" Fermi kissed his fingertips "—perfecto."

"Down!" Luke shouted.

Before she had a chance to react, he'd thrown himself on top of her and Fermi, dragging them both to the snow and covering them with his body.

From faraway, there was the sharp crack of a rifle being fired. She heard the thud of a bullet hitting the barracks behind them.

The two soldiers who had been guarding them moved into position and returned fire.

Cautiously, Shana lifted her chin from the snow and peered up into the forested slope leading into camp. She couldn't see the person who'd fired at them. When she tried to rise, she couldn't move. Luke ordered, "Keep your head down."

His muscular thigh pinned her to the ground. He had saved her life. Again. Rescuing her was turning into a full-time occupation for him.

While barking orders at his men, he yanked her and Fermi to their feet and hustled them into the main building. Inside, he brushed the snow from her shoulders. "Are you all right?"

She nodded, aware that her heart was beating faster. Camp Hale was turning out to be a dangerous place for her. Either she was going to be locked up as a spy or someone was going to shoot her.

They rushed up a staircase to the second floor and entered a large room with a conference table. Two other men stood in front of a blackboard that was covered with mathematical equations. Their eyes were watchful. Their manner, tense. One of them asked, "What happened?"

"Sniper," Luke said. "Don't leave this room. Stay away from the windows."

As he turned on his heel and left, the enormous implications of the sniper attack sank into Shana's consciousness. What if Fermi had been shot? Or killed? The Manhattan Project was only a few months away from the first test in Alamogordo. If Fermi wasn't there to oversee the final stages, the project might fail. History would be changed.

Fermi smoothed his thinning hair across his forehead. He seemed little affected by the fact that someone had been shooting at him. In Italian, he muttered a curse. "I suppose this means there will be no skiing today."

"Probably not," Shana said. "The risk is too great."

He led her toward the other two men and introduced them: Dr. Schultz and Dr. Douglas. Both wore thick glasses. Both had the distracted air of men who spent more time thinking than working out.

Fermi added, "Dr. Douglas is a physicist. He is very interested in theories of time."

A shy grin twitched the corner of his mouth, and his long face brightened as he shook her hand. "Call me Dougie."

"Tell me, Dougie. What do you think of time travel?"

"Interdimensional reality." He gave a curt nod. "Relative planes of existence. And psychology."

"Okay." She had no idea what he was talking about. "How does psychology relate to time travel?"

"You've heard the phrase *living in the past,*" he said. "Sometimes, when we think about past events, they seem real. We recall details— very specific sounds and smells—that were not evident at the time they happened."

"But those are memories," she said.

"Are they? Isn't it possible that we have actually returned to a prior event?"

With a glance toward Dr. Fermi, she said, "Anything is possible."

Dougie nodded. "There's so much more to learn. We haven't yet begun to explore the nonlinear functions of the brain."

Though Shana didn't exactly understand, she was encouraged. The sheer brainpower generated among the three men in this room was enough to move mountains and possibly return her to her own century.

"Good news," Dr. Fermi announced to his colleagues. "We no longer need to wait for the geologist from Denver. Miss Parisi can take his place."

"Excellent," Schultz said. "We can complete our analysis of tuballoy from the four sites and return to Los Alamos by the weekend."

"I've never heard of tuballoy," she said. "Is it a mineral?"

Fermi studied her intently for a moment before he spoke. "Tuballoy is a code name. I wonder how much I can trust you, Miss Parisi."

Again, she was faced with the dilemma of having no one in this time period who could vouch for her. She could only rely on herself.

Shana straightened her shoulders and spoke in a clear voice. "If there's anything I can do to help you in your work, to help you end this terrible war, I'm ready, willing and able."

He glanced at the other two men, then back to her. "I believe you."

His vote of confidence touched her. Unfortunately, she didn't think it would be so easy to convince Luke.

LUKE STALKED DOWN the second-floor corridor of the main house with Shana following close behind. They turned the ninety-degree corner leading to the uninhabited south wing.

He had a couple of hard decisions to make. Fermi had outlined his plan to use Shana to provide the expert geological analysis at the four mine sites. If she was a spy, they'd be handing over valuable information to her. But Shana's involvement wasn't the worst of Luke's worries. He couldn't think of a safe way to transport Fermi across the open countryside to the mines while there was a sniper in the area. "This is one hell of a SNAFU," he muttered.

"A what?"

"SNAFU," he repeated. "Situation Normal: All Fouled Up."

Shoving open the door to a bedroom, he marched inside and unceremoniously dumped Shana's knapsack and skis on the floor beside the three-drawer knotty pine dresser. "You'll be staying here."

She glanced at the bare whitewashed walls of the small square room. The only window was covered with blinds. "Am I a prisoner?"

"You'll be watched." He didn't like having her here. She was a problem, a possible security risk. And he was damn sure she didn't have amnesia.

Casually, she sauntered over to the bed, leaned down and pushed against the mattress with both hands. She frowned. "Hard as a cement slab."

"Government issue," he said. "In case you haven't heard, there's a war going on. Luxury is not a top priority."

She perched on the edge of the bed, crossed her long legs and looked up at him though her thick black lashes. Though he doubted that her intentions were sexual, his mind went in that direction. Their night together had been unforgettable. Too easily, he remembered her arms wrapped tightly around him, could almost see the way she'd leaned toward him, filled with longings and desires as great as his own.

"Thank you," she said, "for saving my life again."

"The sniper wasn't aiming at you."

Twin frown lines creased her brow. "Do you think he was after Dr. Fermi?"

"Yes."

"Luke, it's very important that you protect him."

Just what he needed. More of her so-called "expert advice." For a woman, she was damned pushy, not a bit hesitant to give orders. "Do me a favor, Shana. Don't tell me how to do my job."

"If anything happens to Fermi, the course of history will be forever changed." There was an urgency in her voice. "Don't ask me how I know, but I do."

Her dark eyes glittered with a passion that had nothing to do with sex. This fire came from the soul of a true believer. A fanatic. Who was she? Why had she come here?

He took out his pack of Lucky Strike cigarettes and tapped one out. Before he could light up, she said, "I'd appreciate if you didn't smoke in my bedroom."

"Fine." He returned the cigarette to the pack. "If I'm going to give the go-ahead on Fermi's plan to take you along on his visits to the mine, I'm going to need some answers, Shana. And I need them now."

"There's only one thing that's important. I promise that we're on the same side."

"Prove it," he challenged. "You show up here without valid identification or credentials. Then you cozy up to Dr. Fermi, gushing over him as if he was Clark Gable or Fred Astaire."

"Enrico Fermi is much more important than a movie star. I've always found intelligence to be more attractive than a pretty face."

"Beauty and brains," he muttered. "And a pain in the rear."

"Dr. Fermi trusts me."

"He's not making the decision or giving the orders. I am."

"What about Captain Hughes?"

Captain Verne Hughes presented another problem for Luke. Though Hughes was in charge, he'd become careless, lackadaisical—a yardbird putting in his time until his final discharge came through.

When Luke reported the sniper attack to Hughes, the captain issued no direct orders. All he offered was a vague promise to step up the security. "The captain put me in charge of the visits to the mine sites."

"Mission impossible," she said. "How are you going to protect Fermi from a sniper?"

"Hell if I know." He crossed to the window and peered out at the snow-covered forest. A dozen snipers could be hiding in those trees, behind those boulders. The best way to protect Fermi and his two colleagues was to keep them inside the borders of Camp Hale, which went counter to their plan for visiting the mining operations.

"I can help," Shana said.

"Not unless you've got an extra battalion tucked inside your bra."

"I have a plan." She left the bed and came toward him. "From what Fermi told me, he needs to go to four mines in the area. Is that right?"

He nodded.

"Let me go in his place. I'll take the necessary samples, get all the information he needs and report back to him with my results. You can keep him here, under heavy guard, and then send him back to Los Alamos where he belongs."

When he turned toward her, she was standing close. A ray of sunlight shimmered in her thick black hair. "How do you know what he needs?"

"He told me," she said simply.

If she was a spy, Fermi had already said too much. There was no putting that genie back in the bottle. Her plan, however, offered a decent solution to the logistical problem of keeping Fermi safe. "Much as I hate to admit it, that's a halfway decent plan."

"I'm good at logic." Her full lips parted in a too-innocent smile that made him think she was up to something. "You know it's not safe to send Fermi out there with a sniper on the loose."

If he took her to gather the samples, Fermi and his colleagues would be safe. On the other hand, he might be compromising national security by taking her on this mission, handing over a vital piece of intelligence to the enemy. "What's in it for you?"

"Maybe you'll stop suspecting me." She took another small step closer. "I'm not a spy. You should know that."

"Because we almost slept together?"

Her cheeks colored with a rosy flush. "Believe me, Luke, I regret that indiscretion as much as you do."

"Indiscretion? That's a ladylike word."

He could see the hurt in her eyes, but she didn't back off. "Think about what happened before we were in your cabin. The fall I took on the slope. The hypothermia. The altitude sickness. You know I wasn't faking those symptoms."

"So?"

"If I was a spy, would I have nearly killed myself to meet you? How could I have known that you'd come along in the nick of time? Our meeting was purely accidental."

"I believe we met by accident, but I'm not your target. Fermi is." And she'd gone after him like a vampire to an open vein. "I'm just a G.I. you bumped into along the way."

"You're much more than that." She turned

on her heel and walked away from him. "I hope you'll take my plan under consideration. Neither of us want to put Dr. Fermi in danger."

He caught hold of her arm and spun her around to face him again. Every instinct in his body urged him to taste her lips, to hold her tight and feel her hips grinding against him. "If you're lying to me, Shana, I'll make you pay."

"I'm not lying."

"Simple question. Where were you born?"

"New York City."

"Where did you grow up?"

"All over the world. My father is a diplomat."

At last, he had a straight answer from her. "Call him. Call your father and he can vouch for you."

"I can't. He's nowhere I can reach him."

She pulled her arm away from him and took a step back, retreating into cool secrecy. There was something she wasn't telling him. Something big.

Quietly, he said, "You know, Shana, treason is punishable by death."

Instead of fear, he saw sadness in her eyes.

...and sadness. With all his heart,
...d to trust her, but he just wasn't that
...fool.

Chapter Five

Forty-five minutes into the drive, Shana began to think her plan wasn't such a great idea after all. The four-person jeep had no shock absorbers and no seat belts, and their route led from one rutted dirt road to another. Every time she found a comfortable position, Luke crashed into another pothole. From the backseat, she glared daggers into the back of his helmet.

Seated beside her was Private First Class Henry Harrison. Every ten minutes or so, he'd jolt to alertness, sight down the barrel of his rifle and aim into the forests like a kid playing at soldier. Shana silently prayed that PFC Henry Harrison would never see action on the front lines.

The guy she'd called Moe—whose real

name was Edward Martin—sat in front beside Luke and droned on with a whiny monologue about food. He complained about the powdered eggs for breakfast and the split pea soup—which he called split puke—for lunch. Mostly, he discussed his ideas for improving the tasteless K rations. Apparently, Martin had been a chef before he was conscripted into the army.

Luke eased up the final approach and parked. "We're here."

Creaking like a hundred-year old-woman, she climbed out of the jeep, took a few steps, groaned and stared up the hillside to the site of the first uranium mine where she would take samples. This location was at a considerably lower elevation than Camp Hale. Here the snow was mostly melted, leaving broad patches amid wide swathes of gooey mud, gravel and tailings from the mine.

Shana didn't mind getting dirty, but she was glad she wouldn't ruin her own clothes. Luke had insisted that she change into G.I. gear, including poorly fitted combat boots. Apparently, he thought she'd be less obvious if she looked like a troll.

"Tired?" he asked in a mocking tone.

"Wiped out." She pressed her fist into the small of her back and stretched her aching muscles. "You guys are trained to survive in rugged conditions. I'm only a geologist with a sore bottom."

"Want me to massage it for you?"

She looked up sharply. Was he actually being friendly? Joking around? "I doubt you could find my bottom inside these baggy clown pants."

"I could try."

He almost grinned, and she was glad to see that his attitude toward her might be improving. Earlier, he'd sounded as if he was ready to march her out in front of a firing squad.

Young Henry Harrison and Martin shuffled up beside them. A couple of sad sacks, they muttered back and forth.

"Gentlemen." Luke shot a harsh glare at his troops. "We might not be at the front lines. We might be stuck here in these god-forsaken, frozen mountains. But we're still soldiers of the 10th Mountain Division. Start acting like you give a damn."

With an effort, the two G.I.'s straightened

their shoulders and gave weary salutes. In unison, they said, "Yes, sir."

He turned to Shana. "Do you have your equipment?"

Though tempted to give him her own smart-aleck salute, Shana held back. She was grateful that he'd taken her suggestion and kept Dr. Fermi safe at the base. "There's a case in the backseat."

"Get it, Martin."

They proceeded up the hill to the mine's entrance, where a small crew was finishing up their work for the day. Shana wished she had her modern equipment for testing the soil and the ore. The scientific tools from 1945 were too rudimentary for a real analysis of potential quantity and quality of the uranium being mined. Not that it mattered.

She was already certain that results would show this mine and all the others in the Leadville area were unlikely to produce sufficient quantities of weapons-grade ore. The primary mineral being mined here was vanadium, which was used as an alloy in steel production.

Her work at this mine was little more than window dressing to keep Fermi happy and safe. However, when she talked to the supervisor at this mine, she asked all the right questions and jotted down information, which she immediately passed to Martin.

Before they'd set out on this mission, Luke had informed her that she would turn over everything—every single thing. And he was watching her with an eagle eye, still laboring under the delusion that she was some kind of dangerous secret agent.

Shana decided it was time for a bit of payback. After she had the information she needed, she slapped a miner's hat with a light in front onto her head and turned to Luke. "Let's go."

"Where?"

"To check out the interior and take my own samples." She smiled at the mine operator. "You don't mind, do you?"

"Not a bit, ma'am." He glanced over his shoulder at his crew who were loading into the back of two pickup trucks. "We're about done for the day, but we can wait."

"You can go on ahead," she said. "We don't need an escort into the mine. I'll shut down the generator when we leave."

He hesitated for less than a minute; the man looked exhausted, ready to head for home. The rest of his crew was calling to him from the back of the truck. "Okay by me. I hope you find what you're looking for in our mine. We're always happy to help the war effort."

As Shana watched him head for the truck, she marveled at the difference between 1945 and modern day. In this era, the mine supervisor showed no fear of litigation. OSHA hadn't been established. Protocol was casual.

Though she liked the simplicity, she was also aware that the safety standards for dealing with radioactive dust were nearly nonexistent.

"Sir," Henry said, "I don't think I should go inside that mine."

"How come?" Martin asked. "Scared of the dark?"

"No." His chin quivered. "It just seems to me that somebody ought to be keeping watch outside."

"Fine," Luke said. "Henry stays outside. Martin, you follow Shana and carry everything she hands to you."

"There better not be heavy lifting," he muttered.

Luke took off his helmet, put on his miner's hat and stepped up beside her. "Lead the way."

"That was quick." She arched an eyebrow. "You move very well for somebody with a stick up his ass."

"You've got a smart mouth, Shana."

"I'm smart all over. *Bella e brillante.*"

And she couldn't wait to pull him into the depths of the mine. Very few people—even those without claustrophobia—were comfortable with their first trip into the confines of a mining operation. She'd enjoy watching him sweat.

As she directed Luke and Martin into the earthen tunnel lit by a string of lights, she made sure to mention the dangers. "These wood supports are holding up thousands of tons of hard-packed earth—the weight of a whole mountain. Hard to believe, isn't it?"

"It's cold," Martin whined.

"Ice-cold. Like being buried alive," she said cheerfully. "Don't worry if you have trouble breathing. There's not much oxygen in here."

In response to her suggestion, Martin gasped. "Can't you hurry up?"

"Nervous?" she asked.

"I don't want to be buried alive."

When Martin pawed at the collar of his jacket, she took pity on him. Though he was overbearing, she had no vendetta against him.

She pointed to a large rock that rested against the wall of the narrow horizontal corridor. "Take that stone outside and wait for us."

Predictably, he complained, "That rock has to weigh forty pounds."

"Do it," Luke said.

Clumsily, Martin hefted the stone and staggered toward the entrance. She was alone with Luke who seemed utterly unperturbed when the stillness of the mine wrapped around them. "We should go deeper," she said.

"I'll follow you."

From the front of the mine, she heard Martin and Henry talking, but their voices faded as she went deeper. Using a handheld pick, she chipped off a few samples from the vein.

"What kind of rocks are those?" Luke asked.

"The shiny black is vanadium. The brownish-yellow indicates uranium. If we're lucky we might even find autinite. It's bright, kind of like crystal."

She placed the samples into the container Luke was carrying. He was stooped over to keep from bumping his head against the support beams. Mining was especially hard work for a tall person. "Does it bother you?" she asked. "Being trapped in here?"

"I like watching you work."

Again, his tone seemed friendly. "Be careful, Luke. It almost sounds like you don't hate me."

"Hate is a strong word."

"And love?" As soon as she spoke, Shana regretted the word. Quickly, she added, "Not that love has anything to do with you. Or me. Or us. Definitely not us."

Though she'd dragged Luke into the mine to make him uncomfortable, she was the one who babbled nervously. Being alone with him seemed to throw her completely off balance. She couldn't decide whether to punch him in the nose or grab him and kiss him like crazy.

He leaned against the sandstone wall of the mine and lowered himself to the earth floor. "Come over here and sit with me."

"Why?"

"Because I can't stand up in this tunnel without getting a crick in my neck."

"Fair enough." She edged to the wall beside him and sat with her back against the wall. Removing her miner's hat, she smiled. Being here, inside the earth, Shana was in her element. The silence cradled her. The string of lights inside the mine gave enough illumination to soften Luke's rugged features with gentle shadow. In here, she felt strong enough to handle anything he might throw at her.

"You've got a secret, Shana. And I want to know what it is."

She exhaled a long sigh. "Can we quit talking about me? Just for a minute? You've got secrets, too."

"Not really. I'm a simple guy. A soldier."

"In the cabin," she said, "there was a photograph. A young boy. On the back it said Roberto. Christmas, 1944. Who is he?"

He took off his miner's hat, rested it on his

lap and ran his fingers through his sandy brown hair. "Roberto is a scrappy little kid I met in Italy. An orphan."

She nodded, encouraging him to continue. "In 1944. Last year. Why were you there?"

"I shipped out in November, ahead of the other men in the 10th Mountain Division, as part of an advance team. It was my job to help the brass assess the situation. Five divisions of Nazis were holding the mountain area in Italy. I joined the battle in a village called Lucoe. We chased off the Germans and liberated an orphanage. All the kids found relatives or family friends to stay with. Except for one. Roberto. His father was a traitor, and no one would take him into their home."

While Luke spoke, he stared straight ahead. His voice was calm. His emotions, controlled.

"For some reason, Roberto attached himself to me. He didn't speak much English, and I don't know much Italian. But we communicated. He reminded me of my fiancée's little brother."

"Fiancée? Are you engaged?"

"Not anymore. I got my 'Dear John' letter just before I went to Italy."

"Sorry," she said. "High school sweetheart?"

"Never finished high school. I left home when I was sixteen. During the Great Depression."

She was struck with the realization that his life had been so different from hers. His era shaped him into a man unlike anyone else she knew. "What did you do when you were sixteen?"

"Went to work in one of the forestry service programs in Colorado. A dollar a day and all the food I could eat." His features softened as he remembered. "Best time I had in my whole life."

"Is that where you met your fiancée?"

"It was later than that, after I'd joined the 10th." He shrugged. "It wasn't a big surprise when she ended our engagement. I hadn't seen her in over eight months, and she's a real pretty woman. Fluffy and blond."

"Not like me," Shana said.

"Maybe the direct opposite to you," he

said with a grin. "She's short. You're kind of tall. She couldn't stop talking. You have a lot of secrets."

Their conversation was veering off track, leading back toward her, and Shana wanted to know more about him. "Tell me what happened to Roberto."

"He followed me around like a puppy dog, and I broke dozens of regulations to keep him close and safe. For Christmas, I gave him a toothbrush, and he acted like it was the best gift he ever got. When the rest of the 10th Mountain Division arrived in January, I had my orders to join them. I left Roberto with a priest in a small town. And I promised the kid that I'd come back for him."

Shana could guess what happened next. She remembered the scars on his shoulder and torso. "Then you were wounded and sent back here."

He nodded. "I'm going back for him. For Roberto. That's one promise I intend to keep."

She felt so close to Luke at this moment. Without saying a word, she reached over and took his hand, lacing her fingers through his and giving a light squeeze.

Making a human connection in times of war was a risky business, and she understood why he'd been in such a hurry to leave the morning after what had almost been their night of passion. If he never got close to her, he would never experience the inevitable pain of their separation.

Of course, she would have to leave him. Shana couldn't stay here in 1945.

"Sergeant?" Martin yelled down the mine tunnel. "Sergeant, when are you going to be done?"

He gazed down at her. Lightly, he kissed her forehead, then he plopped her miner's hat back on her head. "We need to get back."

"I guess so," she said reluctantly.

"You owe me a secret, Shana."

And she wanted to tell him. More than anything, she longed to confide, to share her dilemma with Luke. In his warm blue eyes, she saw a hero—a man who could handle anything except for intimacy.

THROUGHOUT THE PASTA dinner cooked by Dr. Enrico Fermi in the mess hall, Luke couldn't take his eyes off Shana. He'd noticed that when she was listening hard to the theories proposed by the scientists from Project Y, she chewed at her lower lip. When she laughed, she gave a toss to her head, sending ripples through her shining black hair.

She was noticing him, too. Several times during dinner, she'd glanced in his direction. When their eyes met, she hadn't looked away. Their gazes linked, and there was a challenge in her directness—a challenge he was ready to meet.

At the serving table, she stepped up beside him and nudged his elbow. "Great tomato sauce, huh?"

"Best food I've had in weeks."

"About my secrets," she said, "I'd like to talk. Maybe after dinner, you could come to my room."

He was ready, so ready. "That could be arranged."

Her eyes brightened. "I'll be waiting."

He liked the sound of that statement. *She would wait for him.* She'd be loyal and true, unlike anybody else in his life. Of course, that wasn't what she meant. But, as he dished up another helping of spaghetti, he felt happier than he had any right to be.

Captain Verne Hughes entered the mess hall and slammed the door against the cold mountain winds. The captain flipped back the hood on his parka. His face was even more drawn than usual. He didn't bother to remove his gloves.

"Gentlemen," he said in a somber tone, "I have news from the front."

A deafening silence fell. Those who weren't staring at the captain looked down at their plates, heads lowered as if they were praying.

"The Nazis are on the run. Our troops are liberating villages in the Po Valley, but fighting continues. Three more men from the 10th Mountain Division are reported dead."

Luke's gut twisted as the captain read off the names of men he had known. Good soldiers. Dead.

With his appetite gone, he shoved the full plate of spaghetti into the tray for the dishwashers on KP. The captain's report had extinguished the brief flicker of happiness he'd felt in Shana's presence. He needed time alone. Time to mourn. Time to consider his own future and his promise to Roberto.

Without a word to anyone, he slipped out of the mess hall. When he was stationed on the front lines, he'd been spared these reports and the sense of futility that accompanied them.

Outside, the night skies held the light of a million stars and a crescent moon. Luke focused on a single distant star—a pinprick of light—and whispered the name of one of the fallen soldiers. Then he named another star for another dead soldier. And another. As long as the stars continued to shine, the memory of these men would never fade.

Reaching inside his jacket, he took out his Lucky Strike cigarettes, fired up his Zippo and lit up. The smoke curled through him, and he exhaled slowly. The war in Europe was winding down. The Nazis were on the run and final victory was all but guaranteed, which somehow made these deaths even more tragic. If only they could have survived for a few more weeks, for a month…they might have come home. Finally.

He stood quietly in the shadow of the mess

hall and finished his smoke. His time at Camp Hale was almost over. As soon as Fermi and the others were gone, Luke would prepare for his own deployment.

The door to the mess hall opened. Shana and Dr. Fermi stepped outside. Like Luke, they paused to look up at the panorama of stars overhead.

Where were the guards who should have accompanied Fermi? Why was he standing out here like a target? Silently, Luke removed his handgun from the holster.

Speaking to Shana, Fermi said, "Someday, man will travel to those planets."

"Yes," she said. "And what will we find?"

"Somewhere in the universe, there must be intelligent life. In an infinite number of stars, the mathematical probability of life other than our own is a certainty."

"Alien life-forms."

"They may already be here, waiting for us to develop the advanced scientific tools to communicate with them."

Shana chuckled. "A paradox. The Fermi paradox. Mathematical probability indicates aliens exist, but where are they?"

"Someday," he said. "Someday, we will know."

Henry Harrison crashed through the door behind them. Only one arm was in his parka. In his free hand, he held his Garand rifle. "You two shouldn't go wandering off. We still haven't caught that sniper."

"I apologize," Fermi said. "Will you escort us back to the residence?"

"Come back inside. We need two people for an escort. Come on. Back inside."

As the door closed behind them, Luke shook his head. Discipline among the few remaining troops at Camp Hale was so halfhearted that it was dangerous. Fermi and his men must be protected; Luke didn't want his last stateside assignment to end in disaster. He needed to discuss procedures with Captain Hughes.

Walking quickly, he made his way along deserted pathways to the captain's office in the one-story rectangular building where he'd talked to Shana earlier today. A light shone through the window of Hughes's front office. Very likely, the captain would be tilted back in his chair, staring into space and ignoring the problems that piled up on his desk.

As Luke watched, the outer door to the office building pushed open. A man dressed in black stepped through. His movements were furtive as he stepped onto the pathway. Was he a sniper? One of the men Luke had been pursuing?

With his handgun at the ready, Luke broke into a run. If he could take this man into custody, he might find out who was after Fermi.

The man in black pivoted and turned toward him.

"Halt," Luke shouted.

Captain Hughes staggered through the door of his building. One hand braced against his forehead. With the other he aimed and fired point-blank.

The figure in black fell to the ground. Hughes lurched toward him. He fired again. And again.

What the hell was he doing? Luke raced to the fallen man and dropped down beside him. He tore open the snaps on the front of his jacket. His chest was already soaked in blood, but he wasn't dead. He gasped.

"Who are you?" Luke demanded. "Who do you work for?"

He clutched the front of Luke's jacket. His mouth worked frantically, trying to speak. He choked out a few words in a foreign language. Russian. He was speaking Russian. Though the Russians were against the Nazis and on the United States' side, that was one hell of an uneasy alliance. Papa Joe Stalin was nearly as dangerous as Hitler—another guy who wanted to take over the world. And he needed scientists like Fermi to do it.

The man in black cried out. A spasm wrenched through him, then his body went slack. He was gone. Dead.

Captain Hughes stood over Luke's shoulder. He still held his pistol—ripe with the smell of cordite. "Son of a bitch. Is he dead?"

"Very dead." And unarmed. His handgun—a Beretta—was still in the holster.

Hughes shouldn't have killed the intruder. A dead man couldn't respond to interrogation. He lowered the man to the ground and stood facing the captain. He was hurt, bleeding from a wound on his forehead. "You're injured."

"It's nothing." Hughes waved him away. "I'm okay."

"What happened, sir?"

"When I came back to my office, he was there. Behind my desk. He held a gun on me."

"Did he say anything?"

"Wanted to know when Fermi was going back to New Mexico. I told him to go to hell, demanded that he identify himself. He rattled off some long Russian name. Said he was NKVD."

The NKVD were secret police; they handled espionage for the Soviets. "He admitted that he was a spy?"

"Yeah." The captain winced and rubbed at his forehead. "He offered me money to betray Fermi. Said it was going to happen, sooner or later. I might as well be the one to get the big paycheck."

"How did he even know Fermi was here? Does he have some kind of inside connection? Was he working with anybody else?"

"I don't know anything else. I charged at him. He whacked me on the forehead and I passed out."

Pathetic! Luke's jaw tensed. The actions of Captain Hughes disgusted him. He'd failed to apprehend the Russian spy, failed to get any useful information, failed as a soldier and as a commanding officer. "Now what?"

"Go through his pockets. Maybe you'll find a clue."

Luke searched, but found no wallet. No identification. In the jacket pocket of the dead man was pack of cigarettes and a matchbook. Luke held it up to the light and read the logo. "Hotel Jerome. Aspen."

Chapter Six

In times of war, regular legal procedures and investigations were sometimes suspended. Luke's job was to follow the orders of his commanding officer, Captain Hughes, even when he didn't agree with those orders.

With Henry and Martin doing the heavy lifting, the body of the dead Russian was wrapped in sheets and carried to an empty shed that had been used to store equipment. The captain locked the door to the windowless building.

Henry shivered; his face paled in the moonlight. "I've never seen a dead man before."

"Get used to it," Hughes snapped. "This is war."

Not really. Luke bit his tongue to keep

from speaking out. *This was murder.* Instead of hiding the body, they should have notified the local sheriff.

"When the ground thaws, we'll bury him," Hughes said. "In an unmarked grave."

"Like he deserves," Martin muttered.

"He was a spy," Hughes said. "An enemy of our country. He was trying to get his paws on Dr. Fermi, to uncover his top secret project."

That much made sense. But why had the Russian been inside the office building going through the captain's files? If he was working with someone else, why hadn't they opened fire when their man went down? Where was the sniper who shot at Fermi earlier today?

"Top secret," the captain repeated as if to reassure himself. He turned to Martin and Henry. "Say nothing about this man to anyone else. Not one word. That's an order."

"Yes, sir," they responded.

Luke followed the captain along the dark pathways in the mostly empty Camp Hale. Last year at this time, the camp had been home for ten thousand men. The cold mountain valley echoed with their voices and their laughter. Every day meant a new training challenge as they pushed themselves to the limit. Practicing marksmanship. Learning mountain skills. Building the teamwork necessary for an elite fighting force.

Now, the 10th Mountain Division had proved themselves in warfare. They were the first troops sent into battle, and they sustained high casualties. The ghosts of those fallen heroes haunted Camp Hale.

At the office barracks, the captain motioned for them to come inside. He shrugged off his jacket and sat behind his desk. Luke didn't like the way he looked. The medic had cleaned the captain's head wound and slapped on a bandage, but that wasn't the worst part of his appearance. The captain's complexion had a waxy sheen. His eyebrows pulled into a scowl above weary, bloodshot eyes. A dark stubble covered his chin and jowls. His fingers trembled as he pulled a cigarette from a pack and lit up.

"I don't think that spy was working alone," he said.

Luke agreed. "This morning, I pursued two men."

"Could be two. Could be more." Hughes took a drag on his cigarette. "Could be somebody working inside Camp Hale."

"One of our guys," Henry blurted. "You think one of our guys is a spy?"

"Maybe not a guy," Hughes said. "Henry, tell me about when you first saw Miss Parisi."

Though standing at ease, Luke tensed as he listened to the recitation from Henry and Martin about their first encounter with Shana on the slopes above Camp Hale. She wasn't armed. She seemed confused. In her knapsack, she carried no identification other than her obviously forged International Driver's License and a plastic card with her name on it.

Henry added, "She said she knew Luke. Sergeant Rawlins."

"Thank you," Captain Hughes said. "Tomorrow, I'll have another assignment for you. An important mission. For right now, you're dismissed."

When they left, he turned to Luke. "What

do you know about this woman? Had you ever seen her before?"

"Never." And he didn't know why he should be answering questions about Shana. They had a dead man on their hands. And a direct threat to Dr. Fermi. "May I make a suggestion, sir?"

"Go ahead."

"Send Fermi and his crew back to Los Alamos. We can't provide adequate protection for them. Not with snipers in the trees and spies sneaking into buildings."

"We got ourselves a real SNAFU, Luke."

"Yes, sir."

"But we're the 10th Mountain Division. We can handle a couple of Russian spies."

Though Luke was infinitely proud of his division, he didn't see this as a matter of honor. "We need to be practical, sir. To file a report on the incident tonight and make plans to—"

"I'm giving the orders." His eyes narrowed. "Tell me about your contact with Miss Parisi."

"The blizzard hit. I saw her fall on the slopes, apparently suffering from altitude sickness, hypothermia and sloppy ski technique. I took her to the cabin where she spent the night and recovered."

"Did she say anything that would cause you to suspect that she was a spy?"

"No, sir. She did not."

The captain stubbed out his cigarette in the ashtray on the desk. During the past month, Luke had watched Captain Hughes slip deeper into exhaustion and a grim resignation. The captain had done too much drinking; he'd shown too little concern for the way Camp Hale was run. Discipline among the troops was almost nonexistent.

With a murder hanging over his head, Captain Hughes was grasping at straws. He muttered, "Miss Parisi is suspicious."

"You're wrong about her," Luke said. "She loves this country. And she thinks Fermi is a god."

"If she's convinced you, she can outsmart most of us. But I still think she knows more than she's telling."

Unfortunately, Luke had to agree. Shana had secrets.

"Here's the plan," Hughes said. "Tomorrow, I want you to go to the Hotel Jerome in

Aspen. Take Martin and Henry with you. Spend the night there and see if you can sniff out the other men who were working with our dead spy."

Luke didn't want to leave the camp. Protecting Fermi was the number-one priority, and he didn't trust Captain Hughes to handle that job properly. "Why me?"

"Because I'm sending Miss Parisi with you. If she's in Aspen, she might try to contact her Russian spy colleagues."

"Sir, I don't think—"

"Don't guard her too closely. Let her think she can wander around. If we give her enough rope, she just might hang herself."

TIME PASSED SLOWLY for Shana as she waited in her tiny square bedroom for Luke. She checked her wristwatch. It was almost nine o'clock. After dinner, she'd been escorted back to the main house by a phalanx of 10th Mountain Division G.I.'s who surrounded Fermi and the other two scientists from Los Alamos. Then Shana was shuffled off to her bedroom where she waited and waited and waited.

Though Luke had assured her that she wasn't a prisoner, an armed guard stood outside her bedroom door. Ever since Captain Hughes had marched into the mess hall and made his announcement about casualties, the atmosphere at Camp Hale had changed.

There was an aura of tension, a terrible awareness that a war was raging halfway around the world. Though they were tucked away in the high Rockies, the specter of those European battlegrounds haunted these men, some of whom would still be shipping out.

She checked her wristwatch again. Only five minutes had passed. Where was Luke? Why hadn't he come to her?

Earlier today, when they were alone in the uranium mine, she'd promised to reveal something about herself. Did she dare tell him the huge secret? The big kahuna? The unbelievable fact that she was from another century?

It wasn't as if she had a lot of options. Literally, she knew no one. She had no money, and ATMs hadn't been invented. No identification. No transportation. Her only thread of hope came from Luke. He had found her, had saved her life. Twice. Wasn't that enough to make her trust him?

Her instincts told her no. Not yet. They'd barely begun to warm up to each other after their conversation in the uranium mine when he'd revealed a bit about himself. When she thought of how he'd befriended Roberto the orphan, her heart clenched. Her mind painted a picture of tall, muscular Luke in his fatigues and helmet, leading an abandoned child away from battle. He was a good man, a good soldier who masked his tenderness behind a macho facade.

But she wasn't sure that his kindness would extend to her. If she told him that she'd been swept away from her century, he might slap her into a straitjacket and ship her off to the nearest sanitarium. She shuddered at the thought of what might pass for psychiatric treatment in this era. Shock treatments? Surgical lobotomy?

She hopped off the square bed and padded to the window in her stocking feet. Though she'd been warned not to stand directly in front of the glass, silhouetted against the light as a target for a sniper, there was no rule about peeking around the edge of the blinds. She saw a couple of men walking quickly along the cleared pathway. Other guards patrolled the perimeter of the building. The heightened security caused the hairs at the back of her neck to stand up. Danger was approaching.

There was a knock at her door. Finally! Luke had come to see her. "Come in."

When he stepped inside and closed the door behind him, she had an urge to race toward him and throw herself into his arms. His stern expression held her back. "What's wrong? Did something happen?"

"You've got to tell me about your background, Shana. I need proof of your identity."

"You saw me working today. Isn't that proof enough that I'm a geologist?"

"It doesn't matter what I think."

"Fermi trusts me," she said. "He said my analysis on the ore samples gave him all the information he needed."

"Captain Hughes is convinced that you're a spy."

Fear took root in her consciousness. She knew what happened to traitors and spies during wartime. The captain had the authority to lock her up in a guardhouse and throw away the key. "What should I do?"

"I need identification."

"There's nothing." Desperately, she tried a different explanation. "Remember how I told you about Kuwait. All my contacts are there. In the Middle East. It's impossible to reach them."

"Even if that's true, you must have luggage. Or a place you were staying in Leadville. A car. *Anything.*" The urgency in his voice worried her. "You didn't just appear by magic on that slope in the middle of a blizzard."

But that was exactly what had happened, though probably not by magic. Shana didn't believe in elves and fairies and magical wands. But the scientific process that had thrown her through time was beyond her ability to comprehend. Like Fermi's paradox. She must have traveled through time because she was here, but she didn't have the tools to explain the process.

Though waves of tension prickled across

her flesh, she forced herself to appear calm as she walked to the bed and perched on the edge. "I promised to tell you secrets about myself. Here goes."

Luke slipped off his jacket and dropped it on the floor. He sat at the foot of her bed and watched her through cool blue eyes.

"I've always been a logical person," she said. "From the time I was a little girl, I wanted to know how things worked and why. I needed answers. My father's career as a diplomat was perfect for somebody like me because we traveled to different embassies all over the world, and I had a chance to explore a variety of different things."

"Interesting childhood," he said impatiently. "But I need to know about the present, Shana."

"I'll get there," she promised. First, he needed to understand something about her. "I guess you could say that I'm kind of a loner."

"I thought embassies were places for fancy parties and social events."

"Not for a kid. I hated getting dressed up. Still do."

"Doesn't surprise me."

"An embassy is like a little island inside a foreign country. Most of the people stay safely inside the compound. But I never wanted to sit at a window and watch life go by. No matter where in the world I was, I tried to adapt and become part of the local scene."

With her olive skin, black hair and brown eyes, she looked Italian when she was in Italy. In Spain, she was Spanish. In the Middle East, she managed to pass herself off as a belly dancer named Aziza.

"Have you ever been to Russia?" he asked.

"No. Why do you ask?"

"No reason," he said. "Go on with your story but keep in mind that I can't stay here all night."

"One of my earliest memories is when my mother was reading me a fairy tale that ended with 'they lived happily ever after.' I wanted to know why. How do we know they were happy?"

"What did your mother say?"

"'Sometimes there's only a dream. Not a logical explanation.'" Shana frowned. "I didn't accept what she said. In my childish reasoning, there were solid answers for absolutely everything. I didn't know about love. Or hate. Or even sorrow. I didn't understand about sadness until my mother died when I was seven."

"Sorry," Luke said.

"So am I." Her mother's early death was an old scar that would never heal. "I understood why she died. There was a rational explanation. She had an untreatable viral infection. But her absence made no sense to me. It still doesn't. How could she be gone?"

Luke reached over and took her hand. The warmth of his touch reassured her. No matter what Captain Hughes thought, Luke wouldn't let anything terrible happen to her.

"Anyway," she continued, "I've spent my life finding answers. Grounding myself in reality. Until I got caught in that swirling blizzard. I thought I was going to die. I'd made a foolish mistake, and I would pay with my life. Then, I saw you skiing toward me. All dressed in white."

She lifted her gaze and looked into his breathtaking blue eyes. "When you rescued me, I allowed myself to be swept away by a fantasy. Unexplainable. Irrational. I don't have answers for you, Luke. Nothing that I can put down in black and white. All I can say is that I'm here. I don't know why."

She wouldn't have blamed him if he called out, "Try again," and shook her until the truth spilled out. Instead, he lifted her hand to his lips and kissed the palm, sending an electric current up her arm.

"You still haven't given me any form of identification," he said.

"I wish I could."

"So do I. I want to make sure you stick around long enough to know what 'happily ever after' means."

"Do you know?"

He didn't answer. Instead, he rose from the bed with a creaking of springs. "Get some rest. We're leaving early tomorrow. After we do analyses on two more mines, we're going to Aspen. To the Hotel Jerome."

"I don't have anything to wear."

As soon as she spoke, Shana remembered that this was Aspen in 1945—a sleepy little village, not a glamorous destination for jet-setters.

"Wear the fatigues," he said. "We leave right after breakfast."

He gave her a wink and went out the door. Once again, she was left waiting. And wondering.

STRETCHED OUT *on the bed, she stared at the ceiling. A huge round light appeared above her head. The glow was incandescent. Beautiful.*

Shana heard her mother's gentle voice. "Happily ever after."

Oh, yes. That was what she wanted. Shana reached toward the light and felt her weightless body lifting off the bed, rising toward the magnificent, glowing circle. The edges trembled, then folded in upon themselves.

As suddenly as the light had appeared, it vanished.

And she slept.

Chapter Seven

After visiting two more uranium mine sites and sending Shana's assay samples back to Camp Hale with two other G.I.'s Luke directed his two-vehicle convoy toward Aspen. Henry and Martin drove the front jeep. He and Shana followed on Highway 82 over Independence Pass.

At this lower elevation, the road was clear—a two-lane ribbon of asphalt that twisted through the forested hillsides. No storm clouds today. Springtime was in the air, and the leaves on the aspen and cottonwoods had begun to turn green. It was May, after all. Across the Great Plains, farmers had already planted their fields. The dahlias were already blooming. The relief of springtime always came late to Camp Hale, but it would inevitably arrive. New life. New chances.

A day like this could almost make Luke forget his frustration about the half-baked suspicions of Captain Hughes and his concern for the safety of Dr. Fermi and his colleagues.

"Tell me again," Shana said. "Why are we going to Aspen?"

"Following orders," he said.

Her full lips pulled into a frown. "But you won't tell me the reason why."

"I go where I'm told."

The captain's idea of playing detective at the Hotel Jerome might produce some results. Aspen was a small enough town that outsiders might be noticed, especially a couple of Russians. But he hated the thought of dragging Shana into a potentially dangerous situation. Though she'd given him plenty of reasons to be suspicious, she had also convinced him that she wasn't a spy. He trusted her.

"I'm not complaining," she said. "I'm looking forward to seeing Aspen."

"Never been there before?"

"Not in this lifetime."

As the jeep climbed, the asphalt disappeared under a rutted layer of snowpack. Up here, it was still winter, and he was glad for the heavy-duty tires that gripped the road. The jeep ahead of them chugged steadily upward, and Luke downshifted and slowed to widen the gap between them. If the other jeep had to stop suddenly, he didn't want to plow into their rear end.

"Why did we take two cars?" she asked.

"Safety. If we have trouble with one, we can use the other. This drive is a little intense. It's better without a vehicle when you can slap on your skis and zip downhill."

"You're joking," she said. "You've skied over Independence Pass?"

"Many times. Part of the training at Camp Hale. For cold weather warfare, you need to build up skill and stamina. This trek provided extra motivation because Aspen was at the end. A town with bars and broads."

She chuckled. "I wonder how Aspen feels about being known as a way station for the 10th Mountain Division."

"The locals are real supportive. A lot of the

G.I.'s are talking about coming back here after the war, maybe to put in some chairlifts and develop the ski industry."

"Word of advice," she said. "Make that investment in Aspen. It'll pay off. Big-time."

Luke thought so, too. Colorado had better mountains and better snow than Lake Placid in the east. Before the war, there were a couple of skiing events held here. "Aspen wouldn't be a bad place to settle down."

"It'd be a great place," she said. "What are you going to do when the war is over?"

Her question surprised him. He didn't often make plans for the future, barely even dared to hope that he would have a life after the war. "Something medical. I could be an orderly. Or a guy who drives an ambulance."

"Or a doctor," she said. "You'd be a good doctor."

"Why do you say that?"

"I've had a chance to sample your bedside manner." She grinned. "And you're smart. Decisive. You care about helping people."

When he was younger, he'd dreamed of being a doctor. But now? "I'm in my thirties. Too old to be starting med school."

"Aspen is going to need doctors. Somebody to set the broken bones when all those skiers come crashing down the slopes. Anything is possible, Luke. Remember that. Anything."

When he was with her, he could almost believe his dreams were possible. Her determination was contagious. With a woman like Shana at his side, he might be able to conquer the world.

"What's the elevation up here?" she asked.

"At the top it's about twelve thousand feet. This highway is based on trails that were once used by Ute hunting parties. Which reminds me, keep an eye open for deer and elk on the road."

She leaned forward and squinted through her sunglasses. The bright sunlight shone on her high cheekbones and outlined her strong features. There was nothing fluffy or girlish about Shana. She looked like the no-nonsense, rational person she claimed to be.

But Luke knew better. He'd seen her caught up in a whirlwind of passion, and the memory brought a smile to his lips. Maybe tonight at the Hotel Jerome he could stop by her room.

"While we're in Aspen," she said, "I want to get some clothes. Some slacks. And shoes. Something that fits."

His grin turned into a full smile. "Interesting."

"What's so funny?"

"I was just thinking about how you're a rational, logical geologist. Then you start talking about a new outfit. Just like a woman."

She smiled back at him. "Being around you is turning me feminine. If I don't watch out, I'll probably want to darn your socks of take up gourmet cooking."

"You'd be cute in a kitchen. With a little Mixmaster. And a Frigidaire. And a pan of fresh-baked chocolate chip cookies."

"No way."

Shana groaned at the thought of herself in a 1940s apron and high heels. Did women in this era really do things like that? Weren't these the years of Rosie the Riveter?

Still, she couldn't deny that Luke's presence was having an effect on her. She had a totally irrational urge to make him happy, to see his handsome face light up with the kind of smile he now bestowed upon her.

When the jeep emerged from the forests above timberline, she was aware that they'd climbed much higher on the pass, high enough to touch the clouds.

Then she peeked out the window over the edge of the road. Big mistake! It was a sheer vertical drop of hundreds of feet.

Her feelings of well-being vanished in a tidal wave of vertigo. On this narrow road, they were inches away from catastrophe.

"There are no guardrails." She heard the nervous quiver in her voice. "Why not? Why aren't there guardrails?"

"Wouldn't do much good," he said. "If you go into a skid, you'd crash through the guardrail. Crash and burn."

"Thank you for that image."

At each hairpin turn, her stomach lurched. The nose of the jeep pointed steadily upward. The engine strained. This had to be the scariest road she'd ever been on. Then it narrowed to one lane. "Oh my God! What do we do if someone else is coming?"

"It depends," he said. "The rule of the road is that whoever is coming downhill is the one to give way."

Backing uphill on hairpin turns? On a snow-packed road? "But there shouldn't be anybody else on this road. Right?"

"Not likely." He glanced toward her. "You're not scared of heights, are you?"

"That would be an irrational fear." She pushed herself back in the passenger seat and wrapped her arms around her waist. "However, it's perfectly logical to be aware of the potential hazards on this road."

"So you're scared."

"A little."

"I'm a good driver," he assured her.

"Unless you go into a skid. Or there's a pile of rocks on the road. Or the jeep breaks down."

She held her breath as he drove across a bridge that seemed ready to crumble at any second. She squeezed her eyelids tightly closed. Next time, she'd ski instead of driving…if she lived until the next time.

When they reached the summit, Luke pulled off on a wide shoulder, stopped and shoved open his door. "Come out here. You've got to see this view."

"Actually, I don't." Her stomach was tied in a knot. She wanted to curl into a little ball and not go another inch by jeep. Could she possibly arrange for a helicopter rescue?

"Get out of the car," he said. "You need to stretch and move around. Loosen up."

She growled at him. "How do you know what I need?"

"Because I've seen other people on their first drive over the pass. You've got the heebie-jeebies, and it's better if you shake it off."

Reluctantly, she opened her door and stepped onto the precipice. They were surrounded by the glacial white peaks of the Continental Divide. The sky had begun to fade as sunset approached. As long as she didn't look down, the view was spectacular.

Luke spread his arms wide to embrace the entire vista. "Top of the world."

Stiffly, she nodded. Her gaze scanned the road they'd just ascended. One hellacious curve after another. The drop was hundreds, possibly thousands, of feet straight down. Then she saw something unexpected. She pointed. "Somebody else is on the road."

Luke stood beside her and stared down at the big, heavy, black sedan. "They're moving a lot faster than we were."

"What kind of car is that?"

"Studebaker." He turned and looked for the other jeep that had gone before them. "Martin and Henry are already out of sight."

She sensed his apprehension. "What's going on? Is that car following us?"

"I'm not sure. They might be perfectly innocent." He turned to her. "In case they aren't, you'd better drive."

"Me?" she squeaked. "You want me to drive?"

"You know how to drive, don't you?"

"Of course." She'd driven plenty of jeeps in Kuwait and Thailand. "But this road isn't—"

"You drive," he said. "If there's a sniper in that vehicle, I need to be free to return fire."

Behind her sunglasses, Shana blinked rapidly. Ever since she saw him exchanging gunfire with the other skiers outside Camp Hale, she'd been aware of the potential for danger. Not until this moment did her fear seem real. A sniper?

"Shake a leg," he said. "They're approaching fast."

When she slid into the driver's seat, her

heart fluttered in panic. Her hands trembled on the steering wheel. This treacherous mountain pass was not the place for a high-speed chase.

"Take your time," he said. "We'll make it."

When his hand rested on her shoulder, his strength and confidence surged through her. *I can do this. I have to.*

Driving with extreme caution, she concentrated on the narrow road and the tortuous curves. When she attempted to speed up, she felt the tires begin to skid. "Oh, no."

"Don't brake," he said. "Ease off the accelerator. Ride it out. Keep going."

The next twist came too soon. She banked to the right, leaning as though her weight could cause the jeep to turn more effectively. Again, she avoided going into a slide. But just barely. The packed snow beneath her tires felt like glare ice.

After what seemed like an eternity, they reached a forested area on the other side of the summit. The wall of trees gave her a sense of security. A false sense, to be sure.

There was still a killer drop at the edge of the road.

"I can see the Studebaker," Luke said. "They're only about twenty yards away."

Then she heard the *rat-a-tat* of a machine gun. The worst-case scenario had just come true. "They're shooting at us."

Luke rolled down the window. Ice-cold wind whooshed through the car, but she barely felt the change in temperature. Her body was on high alert. Her adrenaline rushed.

He swiveled around on the passenger seat, leaned out the window and aimed. In rapid succession, he fired several times before hauling himself back inside.

"Why did you stop?" she asked.

"That was eight shots. I need to reload."

What kind of antiquated weaponry only had eight rounds? "Did you hit anything?"

"Yeah, but I didn't stop them." He glanced toward her. "You're going to have to speed up."

She forced herself to press down on the accelerator, and the jeep leaped forward. At the next curve, she fishtailed. Out of control. *Oh my God, we're going to die.* She fought the wheel and managed to keep the tires on the narrow road.

"You're okay," Luke said.

"Maybe I should just pull over. We could surrender. How bad would that be?"

"These guys aren't looking for POWs. They want to kill us."

"Why?"

"That's a damn good question." His voice was tense. "Is there anything you want to tell me about your past? Anything that might make somebody want to kill you?"

"Nobody here knows me well enough to want me dead."

Though they were still at high elevation, the road was gradually straightening out. There were few trees along this stretch. When she peeked in her rearview mirror, she saw the other vehicle coming dangerously closer.

"Keep it steady," Luke encouraged her. "You're doing great."

"Damn right, I am."

"That's the attitude."

Sheer bravado. In truth, she was terrified.

Tension twitched across her skin like an attack of fire ants.

Across the open terrain, she sped past a few dilapidated cabins and a frozen lake that would have been beautiful if she'd taken her eyes off the road for one minute to look.

Through the open window, she heard a burst of gunfire and braced herself for the thud of a flat tire. Nothing happened. The bullets must have missed. *Don't look back. Just keep going.*

This time Luke didn't return fire. She glanced over at him. "What are you waiting for?"

"It's impossible to aim with all this jostling around. I have another plan." He held up a small round object. "Grenade."

He pulled the pin.

She almost lost her grip on the steering wheel. "Oh my God! Get rid of that."

"I need to time this just right." Seconds ticked by. "I've only got one of these babies."

She was frightened before—now she was deathly terrified. The inside of her head exploded into a thousand jagged pieces.

Casually, he reached outside the window

and gently lobbed the grenade. He counted aloud. "One. Two. Three. And..."

Then came the explosion. Loud and ferocious. In the rearview mirror she saw a burst of flame.

Luke gave a triumphant shout. "Perfect."

What did that mean? She was afraid to ask.

"Pull over," he said.

She slowed to a stop in the middle of the road and turned around. The car that had been chasing them was over a hundred yards away, and the front end was on fire. The hood and front bumper were twisted into a grotesque modern sculpture. Three men wearing ski masks had jumped out of the Studebaker and were throwing heaps of snow on the flames. A fourth man stalked purposefully toward them. He aimed a machine gun.

"Go," Luke said. "He's got a tommy gun."

Shana hit the accelerator and drove into the forest where they were sheltered by the trees. She heard the *rat-a-tat*, imagined a spray of bullets. Squealing around the swooping curves, she kept driving, fleeing, trying to put a million miles between them and certain death.

"Far enough," he said.

She skidded to a stop. Her heart was still racing. Though the jeep had stopped, she couldn't pry her fingers from the steering wheel.

"It's okay," Luke said. "We're safe."

Breaking her death grip on the wheel, she whipped around to face him. "I suppose you want credit for saving my life again. Well, forget it! I wouldn't have been in danger if I hadn't been with you."

Without replying, he got out of the car, walked around to the front and opened the driver's side door. "Come on, Shana. Let's go. I'll drive."

"First, tell me your plan. Do you have any more grenades in your pocket?"

"I want to catch up with Henry and Martin. Then we'll go back up there and take those guys into custody."

"What about me? What am I supposed to do while you're risking your life?"

"Take the other jeep." He dug into his pocket, pulled out his wallet and handed her a twenty. "Go into Aspen and shop."

How dare he insinuate that she wasn't

capable of facing danger! She wasn't a fluff ball in a ruffled apron. Her righteous anger gave her a burst of energy. She charged out of the car and got right up in his face. "For your information, I was required to take martial arts training before I went to Kuwait. You'd be a whole lot better off with me at your side than Henry."

"Is that so?"

"I know how to shoot a gun."

"Ever shoot at another human being?"

"I can do it." She tore off his sunglasses so she could look directly into his eyes. "Believe me. I can kick ass when I need to."

He had the audacity to grin. Reaching up, he removed her sunglasses and gently brushed a wisp of hair off her cheek. "You think you're pretty tough."

She slapped his hand away. "Damn straight."

Before she knew what was happening, he'd pulled her tight against his body. His mouth claimed hers in a hot, demanding kiss.

Gasping, she wrenched free from his grasp. "Are you trying to shut me up?"

"Damn straight."

His blue eyes compelled her, drawing her toward him with sheer animal magnetism, and she knew she should fight him off. But her own fury and fear translated into superheated passion. She needed his touch.

Returning to his embrace, she kissed back. Her tongue plunged through his lips and engaged in a sensual duel. She clung to him with all her strength.

He held her so tightly that he took her breath away. When they broke apart, she was gasping with need. If she was going to die here in 1945, she wanted to die in his arms.

The other jeep chugged toward them. Henry called out, "What happened to you guys? We were almost all the way into town."

Luke caught hold of her hand and dragged her toward the other jeep. Still reeling from his kiss, she sat in the backseat beside Luke, listening while he outlined what had happened to them and what they needed to do next. Something about fanning out and not shooting to kill.

"I want these guys alive," Luke said.

"Who the hell are they?" Martin asked. "More Russian spies?"

"What?" Shana glared at the three of them. "Russian spies? *More* of them?"

"Hey, sweetie," Martin growled, "you've heard of the Russians, haven't you? Commies? Pinkos?"

"But why do you think they're—"

"I don't have time to explain right now," Luke said.

He passed out the helmets and weaponry. When her fingers closed around the cold barrel of the Garand rifle, she forgot about the Russian spy scenario and concentrated on immediate, practical concerns like not getting herself killed. "I've never fired a gun like this before."

"It's already loaded. Just point and pull the trigger." Luke met her gaze. "And stay back. Stay with the jeep."

Henry sat frozen behind the steering wheel. Even when Luke tapped his shoulder and ordered him to drive, he didn't move. His voice trembled. "You used a grenade?"

"Let's go," Luke said.

"I can't." His eyes were watery. "I can't make myself move."

"Martin," Luke snapped. "Take over."

Martin cringed. "Maybe we ought to call for some kind of backup. You know, from the local sheriff."

"We don't have time," Luke said.

"But there's four of them," Martin said. "What if they all have tommy guns?"

"Drive," Luke said. "That's an order."

Martin tromped around the front end of the jeep. He shoved Henry into the passenger seat and seated himself behind the wheel. He drove out of the forest in low gear.

As they approached the smoldering vehicle, it was obvious that they were too late. The Studebaker had been abandoned. Ski tracks led down the side of the mountain and disappeared into the forest.

"This is the second time they've gotten away from me," Luke said grimly. "It's not going to happen again."

Chapter Eight

In the passenger seat of the jeep, Shana stared through the windshield at the surrounding forest and tried to sort out her emotions. *She was angry.* Why was this happening to her? What had she done to deserve being thrown back in time and pursued by men with machine guns? *She was scared.* Beneath her poorly fitted army fatigues and jacket, a sheen of perspiration coated her body. A cold hum of fear resonated inside her brain, sending trembles through her body and turning her sweat to ice water.

Her gaze slid toward Luke. His jaw was set hard as a rock, and his forehead pulled down in a scowl. The range of feelings she had for him defied description. It certainly wasn't logical to be attracted to someone who had almost gotten her killed.

"It's not your fault that they got away," she said.

"Yeah, it is. Like it or not, I'm the leader of this band of misfits."

He had that right. Misfits. Martin—who she still thought of as Moe—should have been in a kitchen somewhere, preparing omelets. Young Henry was so panicked that he nearly wet his pants. And she was a geologist from another century. "None of us are very good at battle."

"I am." He had already been to war, been tested on the front lines. "I should have gone after those guys by myself."

"And probably gotten killed," she said. "You did everything you could."

"And failed."

"Not really. We're all still alive."

"And the Russians are still on the loose. Spies that want to go after your beloved Dr. Fermi."

"When did you figure out that they're Russian?"

"There was an incident back at Camp Hale.

One of them tried to bribe Captain Hughes. Said he was with the NKVD, the secret police."

NKVD must have been a precursor to the KGB. Shana tried to put this information in a context she could understand. In 1945, the Soviets must have been overwhelmed with fighting the last battles of the war, but they still had be interested in atomic energy.

In spite of the intense secrecy surrounding the Manhattan Project, Fermi's atom-splitting experiments would have stirred waves in the scientific community. It was the technology of the future. She suspected these spies would do just about anything to get their hands on Dr. Fermi.

"We have to stop them," she said.

"Hell, yes."

Luke tapped out a cigarette and lit up. When he exhaled a cloud of smoke, she was reminded of an angry dragon. A mythical beast. But that identity didn't suit him. Luke was the hero, the dragon slayer. She wanted to believe that he could do anything.

On the Aspen side of Independence Pass, the snow was nearly melted. Patches of green peeked through the cold, dead winter foliage, and the steep road settled into a more reasonable grade.

Very quickly, the forested land gave way to simple houses on tidy streets. Wood smoke billowed from almost every chimney; the good citizens of this era were unconcerned about air pollution.

When they entered the small town, she felt like Dorothy in *The Wizard of Oz* when she opened the door to her house and emerged into a world of color. This was truly 1945. At Camp Hale, the difference had been more subtle. Barracks were barracks, after all. But here? In the Aspen she'd known before, there were sprawling condo developments and tall hotels. Not in this era.

Without the advantage of artificial snow machines to extend the ski season, the downhill slopes at the edge of town were ungroomed with rocks peeking through the remaining snow. There wasn't even a chairlift, only a lonely T-bar.

The streets—with no stoplights—were filled with clunky old cars and trucks. Not really old, she reminded herself. These vehicles were appropriate for World War II.

Mostly, she noticed the people. Though the cowboys still wore jeans and Stetson hats, everybody else was dressed in vintage clothing and bulky fabrics. A lot of the women had bad perms. Almost everybody was wearing a hat.

Though tension still nibbled at the edge of her mood, Shana liked what she saw. Aspen in 1945 might not be such a bad place to live. She couldn't wait to explore. "I definitely need new clothes."

"Why?"

"I can't very well go walking around in this." She plucked at the baggy olive-green fatigues.

"Who said anything about walking around?" The frown he'd worn since the bad guys got away deepened. "The safest thing is to stay in your hotel room. Those men who tried to kill us are going to be here. They might try again."

She cast a withering glance in his direction. "If the Russians are here, I want to find them as much as you do. There's no way I'm staying locked up in a hotel room while you're out searching."

"Be reasonable. I don't want to put you in danger."

"That's my choice," she said firmly. "Now, what's our plan?"

"*Our* plan?" He scoffed. "*We* don't have a plan."

"Obviously, you came to Aspen for a reason. You must have some kind of clue that made you think the Russians are here. So, I assume we're going to snoop around and find out if the locals have noticed anything suspicious. Am I right?"

"You're close," he said grudgingly.

"I'm coming with you," she said, "after I get some decent clothes."

He parked on the street in front of a clothing store that was a far cry from the trendy boutiques that made up Aspen's modern landscape. Guessing at size, Shana grabbed some black flannel slacks, a soft blue cotton blouse and a pair of black flats. Also, she picked up two pairs of the homeliest cotton underwear she'd ever seen. The total bill came to less than twenty bucks.

The Hotel Jerome didn't look all that much different, except when she got to her room. No television, of course. And the bathroom had old-fashioned fixtures and a claw-foot tub. "Quaint."

"My room is right across the hall," Luke said. "I'll be back here at seven. In an hour and a half. Don't go anywhere by yourself."

"What if I want to—"

"Don't," he repeated. "If I have to hog-tie you to the bed to keep you in here, I will."

"Maybe later I'll let you tie me up," she purred.

Finally, he smiled. His rugged features relaxed, and she saw the man she liked—the man who would someday become a doctor with an excellent bedside manner.

"An hour and a half," he said as he opened the door and went into the hall.

"I'll be ready."

Shana wasted no time in discarding the heavy fatigues and ridiculous combat boots. As she filled the tub, she hummed and thought about Luke.

Compared to men from her own era—men she'd dated—he was more direct and basic. But not simple. Luke had plenty of issues. Unlike a lot of the twenty-first-century men, he was reluctant to talk about them, analyze them and feel sorry for himself. He accepted everything that happened to him without complaint. *Just following orders.* In many ways, he still seemed like a fantasy—a tough, strong soldier who was sensitive enough to care about an orphan boy.

She climbed into the tub and sank low into the steamy water. Oh yes, this was a good thing. After sleeping on army issue beds and tromping all over the mountains, a hot bath felt like silken luxury. Her mind emptied, and she recognized an emotion she hadn't cataloged before. Excitement.

Amid the fear and anger and the undeniable passion she felt every time she looked at Luke, was excitement. Never before had she felt so completely alive.

What if she was meant to be here? This trip backward in time might truly be her destiny. She might be stuck here in 1945 forever. With Luke at her side, that seemed like a very, very good thing.

LIKE SHANA, LUKE HAD decided to change out of his dirty fatigues. People around here respected the 10th Mountain Division, and he wanted to merit their regard. He tucked in his shirt, changed into lace-up shoes and put on a short Eisenhower jacket with a bar of citations and decorations above the left front pocket. Soon he would add the Purple Heart…if he lived long enough to receive the actual medal.

With his hair combed back off his forehead, he checked his reflection in the mirror. He looked spiffy and military—a lot more confident than he deserved to be. Not only had he allowed the spies to escape, but the attack on Independence Pass baffled him. If the Russian spies were after Fermi, why come after him? He was nobody important. Were they after Shana?

Damn it, he wanted to trust her. But every time he got comfortable, there was another reason for suspicion.

Another possible reason for the attack was related to the dead man in the shed at Camp Hale. The Russians in the Studebaker might have been watching when Captain Hughes shot their colleague. Their motive in attacking Luke could be simple revenge. An eye for an eye.

That simple solution would be a relief. He picked up the phone in his room and went through the operator to place a call to an old friend who was on the National Ski Patrol and now lived in Aspen. There were certain inquiries that a local could handle more easily than Luke.

DOWNSTAIRS IN THE LOBBY, Luke hooked up with Martin and Henry, neither of whom had bothered to change out of their wrinkled, filthy fatigues. Their ragtag appearance spoke volumes about their lack of military discipline. Late recruits made lousy soldiers.

"Hey, Sergeant," Martin said. "You clean up good."

"Wish I could say the same for you."

"I didn't know coming to Aspen meant getting all dolled up."

"You represent the 10th Mountain Division," Luke reminded him. "Try not to act like a jackass while you're in town."

"Yes, sir."

He turned his attention to Henry who hadn't looked up from his boots. "Are you okay, kid?"

"I'm sorry," he murmured.

"Only a fool is never afraid." He knew this boy was barely nineteen, a sheltered only child, the son of a shopkeeper in Denver. Henry was a most unlikely conscript. With any luck, the war would be over before he saw battle. "You're going to be fine, kid."

They stepped aside to allow several young people in fancy dress clothes to pass through the lobby. It was Saturday night, and the hotel ballroom was being used for an event. Since the young ladies were wearing formals and their dates were in suits, Luke guessed it was a senior prom. Even in wartime, there were certain rituals that continued.

"What are we supposed to do in town?" Martin asked.

"Talk to the locals. Stop at the diners and the taverns."

Martin beamed. "I'm liking this assignment better and better."

"Keep your eyes and ears open," Luke said. "We're looking for four or five guys. The Russians. We know they've lost their Studebaker so they might be looking for a new vehicle."

"And if we hear anything?"

"Report to me," Luke said. "Do not engage on your own. Is that understood?"

"Yes, sir."

Luke concentrated on Henry. "I didn't hear you, soldier."

He lifted his head and wiped his sleeve across his nose at the same time. "Yes, sir."

"What about girls?" Martin asked. "If we happen to meet up with some girls who—"

"You're on assignment. Not on leave." Luke had neither the time nor the inclination to act as a babysitter for these two. "Stay out of trouble. Get back to your room early."

"How about you, Sergeant? What are you going to be doing?"

"Right now, I'm going to talk to the desk clerk."

"We'll watch," Martin said. "Maybe we can pick up some pointers on interrogation."

This wasn't an interrogation. Luke had no reason to believe that the desk clerk at the Hotel Jerome was engaged in an international conspiracy to kidnap Dr. Fermi. But maybe these two pathetic excuses for G.I.'s needed instruction on how not to be jackasses.

At the front desk, Luke picked up a pack of matches with the same logo as the ones he'd found in the pocket of the dead man. Making casual conversation, he talked to the clerk who recalled several foreign guests at the Hotel Jerome, but nobody who stood out or behaved suspiciously.

The bellboy was more helpful. He remembered five men who stayed in two rooms. "They were prissy about their luggage. Wouldn't let me touch most of it. At least one of them had an accent."

"What kind of car were they driving?"

"A big, black Studebaker."

Those were the guys. If Luke had any doubt, he needed only to look toward Henry and Martin who were nudging each other. *Real subtle.* "When did they get here?"

"Four days ago. I remember because it was Sunday, and I was running late for dinner at my girlfriend's house." He glanced at another dressy couple who swept through the lobby arm in arm. "Looks like I'm going to be late again. Soon as I leave here, I've got to pick my girl up for the senior prom."

"Thanks for the information," Luke said. "If you see those men again, I need to know."

The bellboy leaned close and whispered, "Is this 10th Mountain Division business?"

Luke nodded. "Keep it under your hat."

"You bet," he said enthusiastically. "Have any of you guys been in combat?"

"The sergeant has," Henry piped up. "At Po Valley in Italy."

The bellboy gave him a thumbs-up. "Did you kill any Nazis?"

Luke swallowed hard. He didn't like to talk about combat. Apparently, he didn't need to because Henry had already launched into the story.

"Sergeant Rawlins was at the front lines in the Apennine mountains in Italy with the rest of the troops from the 10th Mountain Division. They were at a high ridge, and the Nazis had taken the high ground. The only direct approach was too well guarded. But there was another way to the top. Straight up. A twelve-hundred-foot rock face."

"That's enough," Luke said. "The boy's already late."

"But I want to hear this. My sweetie can wait."

Luke turned his head and saw Shana standing only a few paces away. She'd changed clothes, and he was impressed by her transformation. Her strong features weren't pretty like a pinup girl, but she was the kind of woman who made a man stop and take notice. Her long, black hair tumbled around her shoulders. Her dark eyes sparkled. "Rita Hayworth has got nothing on you."

"I assume that's a compliment." Looking up at him through her thick eyelashes, she asked, "Do you like the outfit?"

He was very pleased by the low neckline on her azure blouse that gave an enticing glimpse of cleavage. But she was still wearing full-cut slacks. "I was hoping you might show some leg."

"A little too cold for that." She glanced at Henry. "Please continue with your story."

"Yes, ma'am." He shot his hand upward at a sharp angle. "Twelve hundred vertical feet. A heck of a climb. But that's what we spend our time at Camp Hale training for." He puffed out his scrawny chest. "Climbing up and rappelling down. With knapsacks and Garand rifles on our backs."

"Wait a minute," Shana said. "Are you telling me that the 10th Mountain Division scaled a rock face that was over a thousand feet while carrying packs?"

Henry gave a laugh. "It wouldn't do much good to get to the top without weapons, would it?"

"I guess not," she said.

The bellboy was hanging on every word. "Then what happened?"

"Sergeant Rawlins and the other troops caught the Nazis by surprise. There was gunfire, but the G.I.'s kept moving. They spotted a sniper hidden in a nest of rocks that was like a bunker and crept toward him. They had the drop on him, but he got off a lucky shot. Sergeant Rawlins was wounded."

When they all turned and stared at Luke, he felt an embarrassed red flush crawling up his throat. War stories always sounded like the movies where stars were larger than life. Luke never felt like a hero; he was just another G.I. following orders. "That's definitely enough."

"No, sir." Henry stood up straighter. "That's not the end of the story. The way I hear, you were bleeding and wounded, but you still pulled six other men off that hill and out of danger before you collapsed."

"Is that what you heard?" Luke asked.

"Yes, sir."

"Now hear this," Luke said. "Henry and Martin, you have your assignment. Shana, come with me." He turned to the bellboy. "You know what I'm looking for."

"I sure do." He snapped to attention and saluted. "Proud to know you, Sergeant Rawlins."

Luke tucked Shana's arm through his and sauntered through the lobby toward the exit. "Can I buy you a sandwich?"

"I'd love a sandwich." She turned lightly on the balls of her feet and looked up at him. "Maybe a...a hero?"

"Can it, Shana."

"You don't have to be modest," she said. "You ought to be proud."

"I was only doing my part. Like every-

body else. And I won't feel heroic about
what happened at Campiano Ridge until…"

"Until you know Roberto is safe." She
completed the sentence.

That was the bottom line. He'd made a
promise to that little boy that he had to keep.

From the ballroom came the sound of
dance music. The high school must have
hired a combo for their prom. Luke pricked
up his ears and listened. There was a sax.
Drums. A bass. They were pretty good.

"Swing music," Shana said.

The beat sank into him. Oh man, he loved
to dance. His fingers snapped in time to the
beat. He flashed her a grin. "Want to dance?"

"Not now."

"Come on, Little Miss Geologist. Take a
break from being logical. Let's cut a rug."

Chapter Nine

"Cut a rug?" Shana had grown accustomed to Luke's intensity and passion. If he had a fun side to his personality, she'd never seen it. "Since when are you such a swinging hipster?"

"Since now."

His shoulders pumped in time to the music, and he swiveled in a quick spin. She could tell that he danced well. Really well. Not many men could pull off a hand jive without looking silly. Every move he made was smooth, sexy and incredibly masculine.

"Come on, Shana." He held out his hand. "You know how to jitterbug, don't you?"

Actually, she did. When she was growing up in embassies around the world, she'd learned the social graces: etiquette, protocol and how to dance. At her father's insistence, she'd taken classes in ballroom, swing and salsa—lessons she enjoyed almost as much as repeatedly banging her head against a brick wall. "I know how to jitterbug, but I haven't danced in a long time. And I'm not very good."

"You're athletic. You ski."

"And you saw how graceful I was at skiing." Her crash down the slope was nothing compared to the damage she could do to his toes in a fox-trot. "Weren't we going to get a sandwich?"

He caught her hand. With one quick tug, he pulled her close. His other arm encircled her waist. Effortlessly, he guided her in a quick twirl through the hotel lobby and dipped her backward. "You're good," he said. "You just need to be with the right partner."

Self-consciously, she pulled away from him. "We shouldn't be dancing here. We'll crash into the other guests."

"You're right." He pointed to the ballroom. "Let's step inside where we can really hear the beat."

"And interrupt a high school prom?"

"Those kids are so busy staring at each other that they won't even notice us."

She seriously doubted that Luke could go anywhere in Aspen without being noticed. No red-blooded woman could possibly ignore this tall, broad-shouldered man in uniform.

"Later we can dance," she said.

"Promise."

"Okay, I promise. Right now, I'm starving."

Her took her arm and led her toward the exit from the Hotel Jerome. "We'll go to the tavern down the street."

Outside, she inhaled a deep breath of the chill mountain air. Main Street in Aspen on a Saturday night in 1945 was relatively quiet. The stores were closed, and only a few dinosaur-size cars patrolled under the streetlights.

When she shivered, Luke took off his short Eisenhower jacket and draped it around her shoulders. He was being sweet and attentive. *Almost like a boyfriend.*

She remembered the frantic kiss they'd shared after he blew up the Studebaker—a possible indication that their relationship was headed in a more positive direction. Maybe he was ready to trust her, to accept her. She hoped so. She really hoped that the swirling fantasy of their first night together could evolve into something deeper and more meaningful.

With a sigh, she looked up at him. Beyond his left shoulder, she saw the crescent moon dangling like a Christmas tree ornament above the mountain.

As they strolled in companionable silence, he slipped his arm around her waist. Though the top of her head barely grazed his chin, they fit together nicely.

When they entered the tavern, the first thing she noticed was the wildly garish Wurlitzer jukebox playing "Sentimental Journey." The music provided a sound track for 1945. The wood paneled walls were cozy. Like taverns everywhere, the lighting was dim.

Luke chose a round table where he sat facing the door with his back to the wall. Almost as soon as they were settled, a barmaid appeared with two mugs of beer. "On the house, soldier."

"Thank you, ma'am." He gave her a wink.

"When you get a chance, we'd like burgers with everything and chips."

Shana usually hated it when men ordered for her. But a burger with everything sounded perfect. So far, everything about this evening had been pleasant. It almost felt as though they were on a date.

He held up his beer mug in a toast. "Here's looking at you, kid."

"Back at you." She clinked her mug against his. "You sound just like Bogart in *Casablanca*."

"My favorite movie." He took a draw on his beer.

"Mine, too." How amazing! Her reality was sixty years separate from his, but they both liked the same film.

Leaning across the table toward her, Luke said, "I found out a couple of things about the Russians."

She mimicked his posture, leaning forward on her elbows. To anyone watching, they'd look like a boyfriend and girlfriend having an intimate chat. *On a date.* "Talk to me about the bad guys."

"There were five of them. They checked

into Hotel Jerome one day before Fermi arrived at Camp Hale. That means they didn't follow him here from Los Alamos. They knew ahead of time that he was coming."

"How would they find out?"

He rubbed the back of his hand across his mouth, hesitating.

She urged, "You can tell me." *You can trust me.*

His voice was little more than a whisper. "Project Y and Fermi's trip to the uranium mines is top secret. Only the top brass and the people at Los Alamos know about it."

The implication was clear to her. "And one of those people informed the spies. They set Fermi up to be kidnapped."

"A traitor," he said darkly. "I sure as hell wish I could have nabbed those guys on the pass. I want to know who they're working with."

If someone at Los Alamos was a traitor, the consequences could be huge. They could be passing on secrets and blueprints. Shana hated to think what might happen if the technology for building a nuclear bomb got into the wrong hands.

They needed to find the traitor. "Have you got a plan?"

"What do you think we should do?"

She eyed him suspiciously, unable to accept that his attitude toward her had changed so drastically. "The last time I offered up a plan—that I go to the mine sites instead of Dr. Fermi—you did everything you could to shoot it down."

"But we ended up doing things your way."

"I guess that's true." She tried to read his thoughts from the expression in his eyes, but he was much too cool to let his feelings show. "Do you really want to hear what I think?"

He tilted back in his chair and sipped his beer. "That's why I asked."

Her chin bobbed in acknowledgment as her mind automatically sorted possible courses of action into logical sequence. There were times when being a rational thinker was a useful talent. "Since you blew up their Studebaker, they'll be looking for a new car. We should ask around at the local gas stations."

He nodded. "What else?"

"Obviously, they need somewhere to stay tonight. We should check all the hotels."

"Bella e brillante," he said with only a slight hint of irony.

Their conversation stopped when the barmaid delivered two plates with huge, juicy hamburgers spilling over the edge of the buns. The "everything" that came with her burger reminded her that it was wartime and fresh produce was at a premium. The usual tomato and lettuce was replaced by a slab of American cheese and a giant slice of onion, which she removed. She doctored her burger with mustard and catsup and took a bite. Outstanding! There was nothing wrong with the beef.

When she looked toward Luke, he grinned. The soft light in the tavern highlighted his cheekbones and glistened in his thick, dark blond hair. Such a handsome man. On the jukebox, Frank Sinatra was singing "I'll be Seeing You."

"I'm glad," she said, "that you've decided to trust me."

"I always wanted to. You're a strange woman, Shana. But your heart is in the right place."

She wasn't so sure. When she was around him, her heart behaved unpredictably—sometimes fluttering, sometimes aching, sometimes warming with delightful yearning. If she didn't know better, she might think this was love. Shana took another bite of her burger before she blurted out something she'd regret later.

They had just finished their food when Luke waved to an older man who came through the door. He joined them at the table, and Luke introduced Jack Swenson. "The best skier in the Rocky Mountains."

Jack pulled off a knit cap, revealing a mop of steel-gray hair. His complexion was darkly tanned, contrasting with his neatly trimmed white beard. Shana guessed he was in his early sixties—too old for a soldier. "How did you two become friends?"

"Jack spent some time at Camp Hale," Luke said, "teaching us skiing techniques."

"You didn't need much teaching," Jack said to Luke. "With you, I was always saying slow down."

After Jack called for a beer, Luke asked, "What did you find out?"

"Nothing." He shook his head and frowned. "I checked at the gas stations and the hotels. Nobody has been approached by men wanting a car or a room."

"Wait a minute," Shana said. "You were questioning the people in gas stations?"

"And at the hotels." Jack nodded. "Just like Luke asked me to do when he telephoned."

She shot a glance at Luke. Apparently, he'd figured out how to track down the Russians before he asked her to give him a plan. Jack Swenson had already done all the investigating she'd proposed.

A pinprick of irritation punctured her happy mood. Luke didn't care about her so-called plan. They weren't really partners trying to catch the Russians because he'd already decided what to do.

And where did that leave Shana? Was she expected to stand beside him, gazing up adoringly and telling him how clever he was? Fat chance.

"Good work, Jack." Luke clapped him on the shoulder. "If our Russian friends haven't bought a car and aren't staying at a hotel, they've got to have a local contact. Any ideas?"

"I know everybody in Aspen," Jack said. "There's nobody here who would give shelter to spies. They might have broken into a cabin that was closed up for the winter. Or stolen a car."

"It's possible." Luke turned to her. "Any ideas, Shana?"

"Nothing you couldn't think of yourself," she said coolly. No way was she going to get drawn into another fake planning session.

When Jack focused on her, she saw a twinkle in his eye. "Shana, may I ask how you fit into this picture?"

"I'm an innocent bystander who got caught in a blizzard and landed at Camp Hale."

"That can't be the whole story," Jack said. "I haven't seen this handsome young lad in the company of a real lady for a very long time. I'm glad you're together."

"So am I," Luke said.

She wasn't so certain. Luke had been toying with her. Testing her. He'd led her to believe that her opinion counted, then he pulled the rug out. She was beginning to understand why his fiancée had dumped him. He was good at heroics and bad at relationships.

"What's next?" Jack asked. "A door-to-door search?"

Offhand, Shana could think of a dozen reasons why a house-by-house search wouldn't work, starting with the obvious fact that they didn't have the necessary authority to do it.

"If I'm patient," Luke said, "I have a feeling that the Russians will come looking for me."

Shana could hold her silence no longer. "You want to use yourself as bait? Are you crazy? That's dangerous."

"Which is why I'm taking you back to the hotel," he said. "This time, I want you to stay in your room with the door locked."

"If it's too dangerous for me to come along, your plan is definitely too dangerous for you to do alone." She turned to Jack for confirmation. "Am I right?"

"Danger isn't enough to stop Luke."

"But taking risks is foolish."

"Agreed," Jack said.

They both stared at Luke as he drained the

last of his beer and set the mug on the table. "In case you two haven't heard. There's a war going on. Danger is part of the job."

AFTER SAYING GOOD-NIGHT to Jack, they returned to Hotel Jerome. This time, Shana refused to wear Luke's jacket. There would be no casual hugging or hand holding on this block and a half hike. She kept herself separate from him, walking at a fast clip.

"Something wrong?" Luke asked.

"You figure it out."

"Let's see, now. I just got you dinner and a beer. I introduced you to a legendary skier. And I—"

"You jerked me around," she snapped. "You made me think that you actually trusted my opinion when you already had Jack doing your legwork."

"He could do it ten times faster than me. He knows everybody in town, and they're not likely to lie to him."

"The way you lied to me?"

"Not a lie," he corrected. "I just didn't tell you everything."

She stalked through the front door to the

hotel and into the lobby. Ignoring the elevator, she went to the stairs. Her room was only on the third floor.

"Hold it," Luke said. "Where do you think you're headed?"

"To my room where I will lock the door and stay safely inside until morning."

"You promised me a dance," he said.

The music from the ballroom drifted through the lobby. The very last thing she wanted was to dance with him. "Forget it."

He held out his hand toward her. "You promised."

After the way he'd messed around with her, he didn't deserve a dance. Still, a promise was a promise. "Okay. One dance."

Together, they entered the ballroom. The combo—including a saxophone, a bass, drums and piano—was playing a slow dance, and the front man sang something about taking a slow boat to China, which sounded like a good idea to Shana. A slow boat to anywhere that was far away from Luke.

Around the ballroom, dozens of teenagers had partnered up. Half the young men had cast aside their suit jackets. The young ladies in their fancy dresses pressed close to their dates.

In her slacks and blouse, Shana knew she was too underdressed to be here. Also too old. She murmured, "I never went to a prom. My family was abroad during high school."

"We're even," he said. "I never finished high school."

"I remember. You told me." The Great Depression had cut short his education.

"I took all the classes and more. Lots of emergency medical training. But I wasn't in school." He gestured. "This is my first prom."

The slow dance ended with a polite round of applause. The front man for the combo tossed his microphone from hand to hand. "Boys and girls, are you ready to swing?"

The teenagers yelled. "Yeah!"

"Let's hear it for the 'Boogie Woogie Bugle Boy.'"

Luke pulled her onto the ballroom floor. His blue eyes focused on her face, and he gave her a cool, sexy look as he slicked back his hair on one side of his head, then the other. His shoulders bobbed in time with the heavy, throbbing beat.

She mirrored his action.

His hips were loose. His knees were bent as he kicked to the left, then the right. Very cool and hip. He absolutely knew what he was doing. She followed his lead, copying his smooth moves and adding a few of her own, glad that she was wearing flats.

He placed his hands on her hips. "Shake it, Shana."

With hands thrust over her head, she wriggled from head to toe. She probably looked crazy, but she didn't care. The rhythm pumped through her veins. The wail of the sax vibrated inside her. She tossed her head, and her long hair swung around her face. Oh, yeah! She loved the drums, the incessant beat of the drums.

Smoothly, Luke darted close to her and slung an arm around her waist. Without even trying, she synchronized her steps with his. Forward and back. Kick and back. He twirled her away from him, then dragged her back.

"Are you ready?" he asked.

"Ready for what?"

"Both arms around my neck," he said. "And hold on."

He lifted her off her feet and slung her across his right side, then to his left. He was throwing her around as if her weight was nothing, as if she were light as a feather pillow.

Their palms pressed flat against each other. Their heads were close together. And they kept moving, moving to the beat. To the exhilaration of the drums.

When the song ended, he was holding her close. They were both breathing hard. He leaned down and whispered in her ear. "Hubba, hubba, baby."

Hubba, hubba? Who said things like that? And why did it sound like an invitation to bed?

Chapter Ten

Luke intended to drop Shana off in her room and then resume his attempt to find the Russians. It was unfortunate that Jack Swenson had been unable to pick up any useful information on their whereabouts, but the spies had covered their tracks too well.

The way Luke figured, his best option for finding them was to stand in the middle of the street, waving his arms and yelling, "Come and get me." Dangerous? Hell, yes. The intelligence level of this tactic was grade school, but he couldn't think of a better way to draw a gang of bullies into the open.

In the carpeted hallway outside Shana's bedroom, he waited for her to fit the key into the lock. His gaze slid down her shoulders and back, focusing on the lissome curve from her waist to her rounded hips. She had a great little body. Firm and slender. When he'd danced with her, he liked the way she felt in his arms. "Whoever told you that you couldn't dance was an idiot."

"Until tonight, I never had the right partner." She opened the door and turned toward him. Her lips curved in a mischievous grin.

He took a step back. "I guess this is good-night."

That was when she pounced. With both hands, she grabbed his lapels and pulled him into her bedroom. Still holding him, she kicked the door closed. Her mouth fastened on his. Her tongue slid across his lips.

He shouldn't kiss her back. He had a duty to find the spies who threatened Fermi. But how the hell could he resist this amazing, sexy woman?

His hands cupped her ass, and he yanked her against him. Her hips ground against him. In scant moments, the friction of her body aroused him. Desire pooled in his groin. He was hard.

She gazed up at him. "Come to my bed."

"Shana, you know I have things to do."

"Do me, instead."

How could he say no? His sensory memory replayed the intense pleasure of the first night he'd met her. Hungrily, he tasted her mouth. His lips were greedy for more, so much more.

Gasping, he made one more objection. "Don't you want me to catch the Russians?"

"I don't want you using yourself as a target."

"There's no other way." His fingers closed around the delicate softness of her breast, and he groaned with the pleasure of touching her. "If I could think of some other tactic, I would—"

"Stop it!" She shoved hard against his chest. In a graceful, catlike move, she leaped onto the bed and knelt there. She pointed an accusing finger at his nose. "Can't you, just for one damned minute, stop being a hero. You'd rather stay here with me, wouldn't you?"

"Oh, yeah."

"Then, stay," she pleaded. "Leave the job of catching the bad guys up to somebody else."

His vision clouded. He was nearly blinded

by his own lust. "Damn it, Shana. It's not like I have a choice. They came after us. They attacked us."

"But we're safe in here. You and me. Let's forget about the rest of the world. Leave the war and the spies and your duty outside."

He exhaled slowly as he considered his duties, his responsibilities as a soldier. For four years, he'd trained with the 10th Mountain Division. The army had made a substantial investment in his development. He couldn't turn his back and walk away. "I'll come back to you. Later tonight, I'll come back."

"What if you don't?" she demanded. "What if you can't come back to me because you've been shot dead?"

"I won't be."

She sank back on her heels. With her long legs curled beneath her on the bed, she was the picture of seduction in spite of the anger that flared from her dark eyes. Her voice was harsh as she continued, "You can't promise me that you'll stay safe."

"I've made it this far."

"Which is no guarantee that you'll see tomorrow's sunrise. I don't want to hear any more of your lies."

He wasn't a liar. Luke was doing the best he could with the information he had. He didn't know why the spies had come after them on the pass. All he could do was hope they'd attack again. This time, they wouldn't get away.

Reaching into his pocket, he took out his Lucky Strike packet. "Mind if I smoke?"

"Go ahead," she muttered. "Smoking is really bad for your health."

He flipped open his Zippo and fired up. "I seem to be doing a lot of things that aren't good for me. Following orders I don't agree with. Trusting you when everybody else thinks you're a spy. Going to war."

"At least, the war part is over," she said grimly. "You've already been to the front lines and come back."

"I ship out again in less than a week," he said.

Her gasp was audible. She shook her head from side to side as she whispered one word over and over. "No. No. No."

Luke thought he'd already told her, that

she knew he had to return to Italy. "I have to go back."

"The army wouldn't do that. You were already wounded."

"I pulled some strings to get reassigned to the front," he admitted. "I have to find Roberto."

"There's got to be another way. Somebody you can contact. Maybe through the Red Cross."

"Don't you think I've already tried? The priest I left Roberto with has disappeared, and there's no sign of the boy. He has no family. Nobody else but me."

"Don't go." Her voice cracked with strong emotion. "Stay with me. Please, stay with me."

"This is something I have to do."

"But I need you. I don't want to lose you."

Her words shocked him. She sounded desperate and scared. Tears shimmered at the edge of her eyelids. Her chin tilted up, and she inclined her face toward him. In her eyes, he saw yearning and a sincere desire that had nothing to do with sex.

When he'd shipped out before, he wasn't

leaving anyone behind. His fiancée had dumped him, and he'd lost contact with his family. He had nobody back home, nobody who gave a damn if he lived or died. His only family was the army—the other G.I.'s in the 10th Mountain Division. Then, he met Roberto.

Now, there was Shana. How had she become so attached to him?

An unfamiliar feeling crept over him. Fear. He wasn't sure he could handle her needs, her desires, her passion for him. "I'm leaving now. I'll see you later."

He strode toward the door and twisted the handle. When he looked back at her, she was crumpled on the bed. Her hands covered her face.

He should have stayed and comforted her. Instead, he fled. Like a yellow coward.

THAT VISION OF SHANA clung to him as he left the hotel and went into the streets. He'd changed out of his short Eisenhower jacket into a longer coat. In his pocket, easily in reach, was his handgun. If he managed to locate the Russians, he wanted to be prepared.

As he walked the streets of Aspen under the streetlamps, the locals greeted him. People he'd never met wanted to shake his hand and wish him Godspeed. His presence couldn't have been more obvious if he'd painted a big red bull's-eye on his back.

In one of the taverns, he spotted Martin and Henry. Both appeared to be having a good time, laughing and drinking beer. If they'd been more seasoned troops, he could have used their help. Unfortunately, these two guys could barely remember to zip their flies. They'd never be able to handle strategy. Luke was on his own.

Outside again, he counted off the paces on the sidewalk and turned into an alley behind the Main Street shops. Apprehension prickled down his spine. He could feel someone watching. This alley would be the perfect place for an ambush.

As far as he knew, there were four Russians. If they came at him from four directions, he'd have to move fast, to seek cover and aim carefully. Every bullet would have to be a direct hit.

But nothing happened.

He watched the cars on the street, probed the shadows and found nothing. Checking his wristwatch, he saw that an hour had passed. When the hell was something going to happen?

SHANA HAD CAREFULLY HUNG her new outfit in the hotel room closet and changed into the long underwear that served as pajamas. Lying under the covers on the bed, she tried to summon up a fresh burst of anger at Luke. And she failed. She couldn't be mad at him. The man couldn't help being a hero, thrusting himself into danger.

But how could he even think of returning to the front lines in Italy where men were dying every day? Being killed in combat? She wanted to tell him that his search for Roberto could wait until after the war. If he went to Italy next year at this time, she'd go with him. She'd help him find the child.

Next year? Would she be here next year? Or would the time travel reverse itself?

With a mental sigh, she realized that she didn't want to return to her regular life in the twenty-first century. Nineteen forty-five was her time, the place where she really belonged. Here. With Luke.

She turned off the bedside lamp, and her eyelids closed. Tonight, she'd hoped to share this bed—the first decent mattress she'd found in this era—with Luke. Instead, her only companion was loneliness and confusion.

HER DREAM WAS VIVID. She looked up and saw a beautiful bouquet of pink rosebuds and baby's breath.

Her father was talking. His words were garbled as if he were speaking Latin from the bottom of a well, but she recognized the timbre of his voice and his phrasing. She struggled to decipher his words, hoping he had good advice for a change. Throughout her life, her father had only one plan for her: find a good man, marry him and settle down.

She wanted to tell him that he was partially correct. In Luke, she'd found a man she wanted to be with, a man she could never let go. Had he felt the same way about her mother? Mom had died nearly twenty-five years ago, and he'd never remarried. His bond to her must have been amazingly powerful.

Very clearly, she heard him say the words she'd longed to hear as a child, "I love you, Shana."

"I love you, too."

A pleasant warmth flowed through her. Being loved was more important than time or space.

When she reached toward the pink roses, wishing to caress their petal softness, she heard Luke's voice calling to her, "Wake up, Shana. You have to wake up."

But she didn't want to. The dream comforted her.

"Wake up."

SHE OPENED HER EYES. Moonlight spilled around the edges of the closed curtains and outlined the shoulders of a man standing at the foot of her bed. Her heart jumped. "Luke?"

Fumbling in the dark, she turned on the beside lamp and glanced expectantly toward the end of the bed. The figure had moved. The man—a stranger—was right beside her.

His gloved hand pressed tightly over her mouth.

"Silence, woman." His voice was heavily accented. "If you scream, I will snap your neck."

He could kill her in an instant, and she knew it. Her rose-colored dream shredded into shards of confetti as she struggled to breathe. His wool glove smelled like sweat and cordite. He was a gunman, a sniper, a killer. And he had her in his grasp. Beyond her terror, she recognized the horrible irony of the situation. Luke's plan to act as a human target had worked. But the bad guys hadn't come after him. Instead, this man had sought her out.

"Listen to me," the stranger said in a low growl. "You will say nothing. Only listen."

She nodded. When he removed his hand, her gaze searched his face, memorizing his features so she would know him if she ever saw him again, if she was lucky enough to live through this encounter.

His features were average. Dark hair and eyebrows. Stubble on his chin. He wasn't a monster. If she'd seen him on the street, she would have passed him by without a second thought.

Yet, his nearness made her skin crawl. His was the face of her enemy, an enemy of her country, a man who had tried on the pass to kill her. He loomed above her with one of his knees on the bed—a mockery of the intimacy she had hoped to share tonight with Luke.

"You are a spy," he said. "Who are you working for?"

"I'm not a spy." Her voice creaked as though her vocal cords had been paralyzed. "I don't work for anybody. I just happened to turn up in the wrong place at the wrong time."

"Italian," he said. "Your leader, *il duce*, is dead. Benito Mussolini and his mistress were hung in the streets. You owe him no loyalty."

Shana dared to look into his dark eyes. All she saw was darkness. A total lack of sympathy for her. And she knew that this man wouldn't hesitate to end her life. Still she repeated the truth. "I'm no spy."

"And yet, you have made the connection with Fermi. He trusts you."

"How do you know that?" She assumed that he and his companions had been watching from the forests surrounding Camp Hale. Had they come closer? Had they infiltrated the camp? "Who are you? Who do you work for?"

His arm lashed out. His fingers closed around her throat and he squeezed, cutting off her air. "I ask the questions. Not you."

Unable to breathe, she tore at his arm, trying to loosen his grasp. His fingers were a steel vise. Helpless, she was helpless. At the dark edge of unconsciousness, he released her and she fell back on the pillow, gasping.

Her mind hurtled from one solution to another. There had to be something she could do. *Fight back?* Though she'd taken the required training in martial arts before she was stationed in Kuwait, she'd never used her skills in a real situation, never expected to be trapped on a bed with her legs pinned beneath the covers.

"Now," he said, "you are working for me. You will use your female wiles to get Fermi alone."

Her feminine wiles? She croaked, "To seduce him?"

"No. He is faithful to his wife and family." He leaned over her and trailed the back of his gloved hand along her cheek. His touch revolted her. "This time you will not use your raven-haired beauty. Fermi would suspect a ruse."

"Even if you kidnap Fermi, it'll take years to duplicate his research. You're already too late."

"We'll see." He lightly slapped her cheek. "Tomorrow you return to Camp Hale. On the following morning, you will bring Fermi to the edge of the forest outside the main house. My men will be waiting. Do you understand?"

She nodded.

"If you fail," he said, "you will die."

She would never cooperate even if it meant losing her own life. Fermi's knowledge and research were essential to the Manhattan Project, the development of the atomic bomb. Turning him over to another country meant they, too, would have the necessary technology.

They didn't need to kidnap Fermi. All too soon, the Soviets would harness atomic energy and build their own bombs. Proliferation was inevitable.

A cruel sneer lifted the corner of his mouth. A gleam in his eyes suggested that he was enjoying her vulnerability. "You will die," he repeated.

"I heard you the first time."

"If you think this is an empty threat, you are wrong. My men are expert snipers, and we are well armed. From the cover of the forest, we will kill many soldiers." He leaned close to her face, forcing her to look at him. "I think the first to die will be Sergeant Rawlins."

Not Luke. He didn't deserve an anonymous death from a sniper's bullet, didn't deserve to die at all. He'd been through enough.

Her emotions must have shown on her face because the spy said, "You care for this man. You hope to spare his life. Perhaps my men should shoot him now. To show you I am serious."

She swallowed hard. Her throat ached from the pressure he'd applied earlier. Somehow, she had to find the courage to face this man. The only way to protect Luke was to conceal her true feelings. "The sergeant means nothing to me."

"To me, he is a problem."

"Is that why you came after us on the pass? Was your mission to attack Sergeant Rawlins?"

"To eliminate him. And the others."

The others? He must have been referring to Henry and Martin. What could they have done to earn the hatred of this foreign spy? "Why?"

"You are asking questions," he said. "I warned you not to ask."

Again his hand closed on her throat. This time, he didn't apply pressure, but the threat was clear. Though he had succeeded in frightening her, she couldn't allow him to see her fear. Drawing on a strength she never knew she had, Shana shoved aside his hand. "Permit me one more question."

"Yes."

"If I deliver Fermi to you, what's in it for me?"

"You want a reward?"

"Of course, I want to be paid."

Again, she considered fighting back. Her arms were free. She could jam the heel of her hand against his ugly chin and lash out with a karate chop to his throat. But she had no leverage. To make any kind of attack, she needed to change her position on the bed, to get her legs under her as a base.

"Get off me," she said, trying to sound irritated as she fluffed the covers and curled her legs underneath her. "Fermi is a valuable asset, and you need me to get him alone. I want payment."

He stood. "Your life is payment enough."

"Not if I'm captured by the G.I.'s at Camp Hale. I'll be hanged as a traitor."

"You will be taken care of."

He took another step away from her bed, and she saw the automatic pistol in his hand. If she attempted to lash out, he'd shoot her. Any thought of physical resistance drained from her mind. Her only protection was her words. And her logic.

Since he thought she was a spy, she needed to start acting like one. Imperiously, she snapped, "If you're not going to pay me, you might as well shoot me now. I must have a reward."

"You will be paid."

Her heart pumped furiously. Every nerve in her body was tense. With supreme self-control, she lifted her chin and glared at him. "Now," she said. "I demand half now."

His expression darkened, and she feared that she'd pushed too hard. He might choke her again. Or worse.

"You make demands," he said, "of me."

"Earlier, you asked who I work for," she said. "The answer is simple. I'm a mercenary. I work for the highest bidder."

"I understand." He reached into the pocket of his parka and removed a letter-size envelope, which he tossed into the center of the bed.

The fact that he'd had the payment ready and waiting made her think she'd made the right move. He believed her bluff about being a mercenary.

"If you have deceived me," he said, "you will die."

Turning on his heel, he exited and closed the door behind him.

Shana made it to the bathroom before she vomited. With a sob, she collapsed on the cold tile floor.

Chapter Eleven

Luke left another bar and returned to the sidewalk where he'd been pacing for almost two hours. At various times through the night, he'd sensed that he was being watched, but no one had confronted him. His plan to draw the spies into the open hadn't worked.

He spotted someone running down Main Street toward him. His fingers closed around the gun in his pocket, and he braced himself.

"Sergeant!" It was the bellboy from the hotel. His suit coat flapped around his skinny body like bat wings. Breathing hard, he came to a stop a few steps away from Luke. "I saw one of the guys you're looking for."

"Where?"

"The hotel," he said. "Hotel Jerome."

"Checking in?"

The kid shook his head. "Going up the stairs."

Toward the third floor. Toward Shana's room. But that was impossible. The Russians wouldn't know where she was staying…unless she told them.

He turned to the bellboy. "You did good."

"I hope so." He shook himself. "Because my girlfriend is going to kill me for leaving her alone at the prom."

Luke stalked down the street with the bellboy at his side. "Suppose this bad guy wanted to find out who was staying in which room. How could he get that information?"

"It's easy," the kid said. "All you gotta do is call the switchboard operator and ask."

Hotel security was lax. There wasn't a detective on duty. And tonight, with the prom underway, the lobby was hectic, filled with people coming and going.

When Luke stepped through the door of the Hotel Jerome, he patted the kid's shoulder. "Thanks. I've got it from here."

"Anytime, Sergeant."

He took the stairs two at a time. His pistol was in his hand. He dreaded opening the door to Shana's room, fearing that his most dire suspicions were true, that she was a spy who consorted with the enemy.

The lock on her door showed scratch marks as though it had been tampered with. It was unlocked. The handle turned easily in his grasp. Gun in hand, he charged inside.

The bedside lamp was on. Shana sat up in the bed with her knees drawn up and her back pressed against the headboard. The moment she saw him, she threw aside the covers and bolted toward him, diving into his arms with such force that he crashed into the door as it closed.

"Thank God, you're here." Her voice quavered. "I was afraid. I never thought I'd see you again."

His arms encircled her, and he rested his cheek against her silky black hair. He ought to suspect her, ought to sit her down and make her give him the answers. The whole goddamned truth. But all he wanted was to comfort and protect her.

From the first time he saw her in trouble on the slopes, he had sensed that she needed him. A few hours ago, she'd told him as much. She needed him…and only him. No other man could fulfill her.

As her body molded perfectly to his, his eyelids closed, and he realized that he needed her, as well. Even though he knew next to nothing about her, she somehow managed to fill all the empty spaces in his life.

He stroked her shoulders. Through his gloves, he massaged the taut muscles in her back and traced the ridge of her spinal cord. Her frame was as delicate as a bird—a lovely graceful creature who might teach him how to fly. If only he could trust her.

Her arms loosened and she leaned back in his arms, gazing up at him with her shining brown eyes. "One of the Russians was here. In my room."

"Did he hurt you?"

"I'm okay." Her hand went to her neck and lightly touched the hollow at the base of her throat. "I have something to show you."

The moment she stepped out of his embrace, he wanted her back. But he forced his arms to drop loosely to his sides.

She went to the foot of the bed and picked

up an envelope. With trembling fingers, she held it toward him. "That's supposed to be my first payment for betraying Dr. Fermi."

"Come again?"

"That Russian spy, that bastard, thought he could pay me off."

He noted that the envelope was still sealed. "You didn't open it."

"Blood money," she said. "It disgusts me. I'm no traitor."

With all his heart, he wanted to believe her. But the evidence to the contrary couldn't be ignored. She'd had a conference with the bad guys, and they didn't kill her. They gave her money instead. "Start at the beginning."

"I was asleep. I opened my eyes, and there he was." Her shoulders trembled. "He thought I was a spy like him. If I didn't do what he wanted, he'd kill me. So, I lied and told him that I'm a mercenary and wanted money. He must have expected me to say that because he had this envelope already prepared."

"What are you being paid to do?"

"To get Dr. Fermi alone tomorrow morning and to bring him to the edge of the forest outside the main house. If I don't do it, he'll kill me and you and a lot of other people. His snipers will open fire on the camp."

"From the trees."

He turned away from her while he considered this threat from a tactical standpoint. The Russians meant to engage Camp Hale in active warfare—a battle within the boundaries of the United States. A brazen idea. Crazy as hell. And yet, from a tactical standpoint, it might work. Though Luke could move Fermi and the men who were guarding him farther into the camp where they would be out of range from the forest, that meant they'd be inside a maze of vacant barracks. All those empty buildings offered too many places for snipers to hide.

When he was fighting in the villages of Italy, Luke had seen the complexities of urban combat. A small determined force of elite marksmen had the advantage. They could strike with pinpoint accuracy and disappear before engaging.

He circled the bed and stood at the edge of the window. Easing the curtain aside, he peeked out at tne street below. Some of the teenagers from the prom were on the sidewalk. Their loud, excited chatter floated up toward him, and he wished he could be like them. Carefree. Innocent. With nothing more to worry about than a prom.

Had he ever been that young? Even before he was a G.I., he'd always been fighting, overcoming odds. It didn't look as if he'd be getting a reprieve any time soon. "I need to get Fermi out of there. Immediately."

She nodded vigorously. "It's the only way."

Tomorrow morning, he would telephone Captain Hughes and tell him. Fermi and the other scientists needed to be evacuated. "Easier said than done."

"I don't see a problem," she said. "Load Dr. Fermi and the others into a jeep and drive south until you get to Los Alamos."

"There are only three roads that lead away from Camp Hale," he said. "You saw what happened when we went over Independence Pass. The snipers could be waiting for us, setting up an ambush."

"What about a helicopter?"

He could probably get some kind of

aircraft from Lowry Air Base in Denver, but that required orders, requisitions and red tape. The process could take a couple of days. The trick would be to keep Fermi safe until then.

"When did the Russian say you were supposed to deliver Fermi?"

"Day after tomorrow. In the morning." She cocked her head to one side. "Seems weird to do it in the morning. I'd have thought nighttime would be better."

"The guards are doubled at night," he said, "and Fermi is safely tucked away in his bed. In the morning, he's itching to get outdoors."

"So that's a more logical time to grab him."

Though she'd appeared to be terrified when he first came into the room and he wanted to believe her, he had questions. He went to the bed, sat down beside her and took both of her hands in his. "This is important, Shana. Tell me how the Russian knew where you were."

"I don't know."

"But have you communicated with any-one?"

"Of course not."

He glanced at the telephone on the bedside table. She could have made a call when she was up here alone. "The truth, Shana."

"Do you suspect me?" She pulled her hands away from him and folded her arms below her breasts. "I can't believe it."

"I'm trying like hell to believe what you're saying, but you're not giving me much help. I turn my back for a minute, and you're conferring with the enemy. Taking a payment from them."

"You're way off base."

"Maybe so, but I'm sick and tired of playing games with you." He tore off his gloves and threw them on the dresser. "You have no valid identification. You appeared out of nowhere. There's no one we can call to verify who you are."

"I explained all that."

"Amnesia? Contacts in Kuwait? You really expect me to buy that load of malarkey?"

"You know I'm not working with the bad guys." Her fists pounded against her thighs, emphasizing each word. "I want Dr. Fermi to be safe."

"Then tell me the truth." The time had come to tear away all her flimsy deceptions. He unbuttoned his jacket, removed the pistol from his pocket and set it on the bedside table. "People don't appear out of thin air with no history or connection to anyone else."

"What if I did?"

"Level with me, Shana."

She hopped off the bed and paced on the carpet in front of him. Though her long underwear was baggy in the butt, the fabric hugged her slender waist. Her lips twitched as if she was struggling to find the right words. Abruptly, she faced him and blurted. "I'm from another time."

"Another time?"

"The next millennium," she said. "I don't know how or why I landed here in 1945, but it happened in the blizzard. There was all that cold and the swirling snow and the cabin and you and—"

"Stop." He held up his hand to stop the words that spewed from her lips in a geyser of craziness. Of all the excuses he'd heard from her, this was the most far-fetched. The most ridiculous. "You want me to believe you traveled through time."

"It's the truth." She exhaled a quick sigh. "And it's a relief to finally say it. I came backward in time. The birth date on my International Driver's License is accurate—1974. That's when I was born."

Under the sign of the cuckoo. What comic book did she waltz out of? He would have laughed out loud, but her eyes were serious.

"Think about it," she urged him. "My fiberglass skis. My poles and bindings. Even my clothes are made from fabrics you've never seen before. Oh yeah, and the cell phone."

"Weird stuff," he agreed. But none of her gadgets proved that she came from the future.

"The real reason I know about Fermi is that his experiments are a success. He and the other scientists at Los Alamos have built a bomb that's capable of decimating an entire city. The first test will take place in two months. There will be a mushroom-shaped cloud."

"One bomb that can destroy a whole city?"

"That's right," she said. "The war in Europe is almost over. Hitler will commit suicide in his bunker in Berlin. The war in Japan will end after two of Fermi's atomic bombs are dropped on Hiroshima and Nagasaki."

"And the cities are destroyed."

She dropped her gaze. "Since I'm telling you the truth, I'm not sure how I feel about those bombs. So many people will die. What if I was sent back in time to prevent the bomb from being dropped?"

"Right," he said dryly. "You were sent back in time to save the world."

She groaned. "That sounds even crazier than if I dropped here by accident. But I keep thinking there has to be a reason, an explanation. It's significant that I met Fermi. And that I met you."

"Why me?"

"Our first night together…"

Her voice faded to stillness. After her wild ramblings, the silence was sweet relief. He should have known better than to challenge her identity. This was her secret, and she'd never tell him the truth.

Quietly, she said, "That night was different. I've never felt like that before. Swept away. It seemed like a fantasy."

When she gazed up at him through her thick lashes, his memory flooded with images, one on top of the other. It had been a night he would never forget. But he didn't believe in magic or science fiction. Time travel?

"Please," she whispered, "you've got to believe me."

He glanced toward the unopened envelope. Her supposed payoff. At least, she'd been forthcoming about what the Russian spy expected of her. "Here's what I can believe. You're honestly concerned about Fermi. His safety."

"And yours," she said. "The Russian wants you dead. He said you were a problem for him. And he also threatened Henry and Martin."

"You're joking."

She shook her head, sending a ripple through her long black hair. "I wish I was. The reason he came after us on the pass was to *eliminate* you and them."

He couldn't imagine Henry and Martin— a couple of knuckleheads—causing any sort of serious espionage problem. Those two could barely manage to walk and chew gum at the same time.

"We should find them," Shana said. "We need to make sure they're okay."

"We?"

"If you think I'm going to let you go out on the street by yourself, you're crazier than I am."

"Not likely," he said. "Being crazier than you is one hell of a stretch, lady."

"I'm telling the truth."

Slowly, he rose from the bed. "I'm going to do you a favor. I'm going to pretend that you never said a word about time travel and the next millennium. You've got some kind of deep, dark secret. Fine. Keep it. Don't tell me how you got here. Don't tell me why. Above all, don't tell me any more lies."

She actually had the gall to look insulted. "You're angry."

"You could say that." Angry and sad at the same time. All he wanted from her was an explanation.

"No matter what you think about me, Henry and Martin might be in danger. We need to do something."

Her concern seemed genuine. She cared about those two guys. And about him. In spite of her latest and zaniest excuse, she was a good person.

With a sigh, he reached toward her. His fingertips brushed a strand of hair off her forehead and tucked it behind her ear, and she inclined her cheek toward his hand as if she wished to prolong their touch. He said, "Henry and Martin will be fine. Jack Swenson is keeping an eye on them."

"Your friend who's a skier?"

"And a marksman." Jack would probably do a better job of protecting Henry and Martin than Luke. "Don't worry. Our boys are safe."

"If we were in my time zone, you could have called Henry and Martin on their cell phones. You know, the electronic device I had in my pack? It's like a walkie-talkie only smaller. Some of them are no bigger than a credit card." She laughed. "But those haven't been invented yet, either."

"Do me a favor, Shana. Stop talking."

She arched an eyebrow. "Make me."

Gladly, he silenced her with a kiss.

Chapter Twelve

Shana had what she wanted. The truth was out. And Luke was in her bed.

In a roaring frenzy of passion, they'd torn off their garments and scattered them around the room. Across the dresser. On the foot of the bed. All over the floor.

Under the covers, they were naked. And their desperate excitement took on a more subtle tone. For a long moment, she lay with her head on the pillow and merely gazed at his handsome face. He had seen so much and fought so heroically. Yet, she saw hope in his eyes. The facets of his irises reflected more brilliantly than polished sapphires. She traced a fingertip across his mouth, pushing his lips into a smile.

"There," she said. "Now you look happy."

"I am happy. As long as you don't start talking again, I'm real happy."

"I can do that. For tonight."

This night belonged to them; they had earned these moments of pleasure that transcended imminent danger and the impossible fact that she was here in this era.

She glanced down at the angry red scar on his shoulder—a permanent reminder of the ravages of a war he was still fighting. He intended to return to that battle; their time together might be cut short. She stopped herself from worrying about what might happen tomorrow or next week.

Tonight, she didn't want to think. Tonight was a time for fantasy.

He cupped her breasts and teased the nipples into sensitive peaks. Each flick of his thumb sent a thrill racing through her body. His hand glided down her torso and came to rest at the juncture of her thighs. His fingers parted the delicate folds and he stroked.

Shivering with pleasure, she groaned. Her body was ready for him, yearning for him, needing him with a rawness that defied logic.

He mounted her, and she welcomed the pressure of his weight on her naked body. Her thighs parted, and he fit himself into that cradle.

His slow, deliberate movements drove her wild. She writhed beneath him, and when he sheathed himself inside her, starbursts of ecstasy exploded behind her eyelids. With each slow thrust, he heightened her pleasure until she erupted in an elemental explosion, hot and unstoppable.

Barely able to breathe, she whispered his name again and again as if by repeating she could assure herself that he would always be a part of her, inside of her.

Though it seemed impossible to achieve another climax, he took her there. Every fiber of her body quivered, and she whimpered. This was too much. She couldn't take any more.

He exploded inside her, and her mind shattered.

HER EYES SQUEEZED SHUT. She heard a symphony of violins and the cascading trill of a grand piano. The notes separated into music, and she recognized Beethoven. Though she didn't know where the music was coming from, she heard it with perfect clarity.

Her eyelids opened. The walls were plain and square, painted a pale vanilla color. Through the long, rectangular window, she saw the lights of a city.

WITH A BLINK, the vision was gone. She was back in the Hotel Jerome, lying beside this incredible man.

"Did you hear music?" she asked.

"Only the singing of angels."

He lit a cigarette, and she smiled. Smoking after sex was so 1945. "Actually, I think it was Beethoven."

"I heard you." He laced his fingers with hers and brought her hand to his lips for a light kiss. "I like all those little sounds you make."

She decided not to push about the music she'd heard. Telling him that she was from the future was probably enough for one night.

Still, she had to wonder about that auditory hallucination and the quick glimpse of a vision. This wasn't the first time. When she first came to Camp Hale, she'd heard the sound of an ambulance. Earlier tonight, she saw roses and heard her father's voice.

And the circle of light. Very clearly, she remembered that vision when she was drifting upward toward a glowing white light.

These experiences had to mean something.

Luke shifted in the bed beside her, propping himself up on one elbow. "Just suppose that you really were from the next millennium. Would you want to go back?"

"There are things I like about my time," she admitted. "The technology is a lot better. Personal computers. Digital cameras. Televisions have hundreds of channels."

"What about medicine?"

"Of course, the vaccines have improved and some diseases have been completely eradicated." How could she sum up sixty years of advances in medicine? "The most remarkable thing has to be the transplants. Diseased organs can be replaced."

"Like a heart?"

"Heart transplants are common. And kidneys and lungs."

"Interesting."

She could hear disbelief in his voice, and she didn't blame him. Even though she was actually here in the middle of a different era, she found the experience difficult to accept.

"Would you want to go back?" he repeated. "Would you miss all your fancy gadgets?"

Her life in the twenty-first century had been comfortable. She had a successful career and enjoyed her work. Her bank account held a very healthy balance, and she was able to purchase just about anything her heart desired.

If she never returned to her own millennium, there were a few people she'd regret never seeing again. With all the travel required in her job, it was difficult to stay in touch with friends. But there were a few girlfriends she managed to meet regularly.

Her family relationships were distant but not terrible. If she disappeared from the twenty-first century, her greatest regret would be that she never took the time to have an in-depth conversation with her father and to mend fences.

"I'd be sad if I never saw my friends again. Or my family. And I was doing well in my career." None of those things compared with the wild, swirling fantasy she shared with Luke. "However, all things considered, I'd rather stay here in 1945 with you."

"Even though there's a war going on," he said.

She shrugged. "There are always wars."

"Even though you're in danger from a foreign spy."

"Being alive means you're always at risk. With you, I feel more alive than I've ever been before."

He leaned down and kissed her forehead. "Same here."

"Obviously, we're meant to be together."

She had a sense that this was more than pillow talk. *Meant to be together. Destiny.* She glimpsed a piece of rational logic that was just beyond her comprehension. If she could only see clearly, she would understand everything that had happened to her.

Then Luke kissed her lips and pulled her close. All logic faded.

AT NINE O'CLOCK the next morning, Luke had gotten his two-jeep convoy on the road, headed back over Independence Pass toward Camp Hale. This time, he went first with Martin and Henry following close behind in their own jeep.

Though the steep, sharp curves of Highway 82 demanded his attention, Luke scanned the landscape, watching for snipers. Beside him in the passenger seat, Shana sat with the loaded Garand rifle across her lap.

"Riding shotgun," she said. "I'm not really sure I know how to shoot this thing."

"If we run into trouble, hand the gun to me."

"And what should I do?"

"Stay out of the way." He hated bringing her back to Camp Hale, back into danger. "Shana, it's not too late to reconsider. I can take you back to Aspen and leave you with Jack Swenson. He's a good man, somebody I'd trust with my life."

"I'm not leaving you," she said in the determined tone he was beginning to recognize. Once she set her mind to something—even something as crazy as her time travel story— she didn't back down. "Besides, I made a deal with those spies. I took their money.

Once they figure out that I've betrayed them, they'll come after me. No matter where I am."

Last night, they'd opened the envelope and found that it contained two thousand dollars. A substantial amount for 1945.

"About that money," he said. "It's better if we don't mention it to Captain Hughes. Or to anybody else."

"Why? It's not like I'm going to keep it."

"They still think you're a spy. They don't know you the way I do."

"I should hope not."

Her amused little chuckle reminded him of their lovemaking. The sounds she made in bed—her whispers, her giggles, her gasps and groans—excited him. She wasn't one of those women who stood by and let him do all the work. Shana was an eager participant; she'd even taught him a few things.

"Believe me, Luke. *Nobody* knows me the way you do."

"I don't suppose you've told anybody else about this time travel thing."

"Not a soul."

"Lucky me," he muttered.

When they emerged from the forested area, he breathed a little easier. Along this open stretch of road, there were few places for a sniper to hide.

The weather today was as temperate as yesterday with only a few wispy clouds trailing across the intense blue skies. Spring-time was in the air. Soon, the snowpack would be melted except on the highest peaks, and the hillsides would turn lush and green. He wished he could spend the summer with Shana, lying beside a rippling mountain stream with her at his side, naked and willing as a heathen wood nymph.

"About the time travel," he said, "that's another thing you should keep to yourself."

"I'd like to talk to Fermi about it. In a hy-pothetical kind of way. I mean, he's one of the most brilliant theoretical physicists of all time. He might be able to give me an expla-nation."

"Be careful what you say," he warned. "And not a word about this to Captain Hughes or any of the other G.I.'s."

"Agreed."

"If Fermi tells you time travel is impossible, will you believe him?"

"Of course not." Once again, her tone was determined. "I'm living proof that it happened. I didn't make up the past thirty-two years of my life."

For a moment, he took his eyes off the road and glanced over at her. Her cheeks were rosy from the cold. Her eyes sparkled, and her full lips were the color of fresh raspberries. She looked sweet and beautiful—nowhere near as complicated as she really was.

He almost believed her story about coming backward in time. *Almost.*

She sat up straighter in the seat and pointed. "There's the burned-out Studebaker."

The car he'd blown up with his grenade had been dragged off to the side of the road. A twisted wreck of scorched metal and busted windows. He grinned. "Oh boy, that's cool."

"It's grotesque," she said. "I'm amazed that nobody was seriously hurt in that explosion."

"Yeah, too bad."

On the opposite side of the road from the wreck, he could still see the trail of four skiers leading downhill into the forest. Because they hadn't shown up on any hotel registries and—according to Jack Swenson—they hadn't made an attempt to purchase another vehicle, Luke concluded that they had a local contact.

He wondered if the county sheriff had come up here to investigate. Though Luke would have felt better about following procedure and reporting the details of what had happened, that meant explaining the spies and why they were sniffing around Camp Hale. Which ultimately led to top secret information about Fermi and his Project Y that Shana had referred to as the Manhattan Project.

Earlier this morning, when he'd talked on the telephone with Captain Hughes, Luke had been ordered not to file a report with the local authorities. He didn't like the captain's way of disregarding the stated laws of the land, especially when it came to the dead man whose body was stored in the shed. Why had that dead Russian been poking around in the captain's office? Why had he offered Captain Hughes a bribe?

Maybe Shana could bring a new perspective to those questions. Though she had some crazy ideas, she was smart. "Here's a hypothetical for you," he said. "Suppose I told you that there was another spy. A fifth man. Suppose he was sneaking around in Captain Hughes's office. What would he be looking for?"

"Official records and communications," she said. "If there was information about troop deployments or strategy, that could be valuable to a spy."

"But most of the troops have already shipped out from Camp Hale. We're down to a skeleton crew."

"Your captain is still in touch. He knew when men from the 10th Mountain Division were killed in action."

"He gets reports after the fact," he said. "But nobody in Europe is going to consult with an army base in Colorado before making strategy decisions."

"There could be some kind of top secret files," she said. "Certainly, there were communications about Dr. Fermi's visit to the uranium mines."

"Bingo," he said. "It always comes back to Fermi."

"That's why the spies are here," she said. "Every country in the world would like to sink their talons into him. His project is about to change the world."

THE REST OF THE RIDE back to Camp Hale was uneventful, and Luke reported immediately to the barracks building where the offices were housed. Though the door to the captain's office was open, Luke had the sense that he was intruding.

Captain Hughes sat behind his desk with his elbows propped on the top and his forehead pressed against his fingertips. He was a mess. As General Sherman said, "War is hell," and Hughes looked as though he'd taken up permanent residence in Satan's realm.

Stepping into the doorway, he snapped a salute. "Sir."

"Come in. At ease." Hughes looked up slowly as if the simple act of lifting his head was exhausting. "No need to be so damned military."

When Luke approached the desk, he smelled whiskey, though it was before noon. His training as a soldier taught him to respect the chain of command, in spite of the obvious fact that his commanding officer appeared to be half drunk and incapacitated.

Common sense urged him to shove Hughes aside and take over the operations of Camp Hale. "Sir, were you able to arrange for an aircraft to evacuate Fermi and the other scientists?"

With a clumsy gesture, the captain shoved aside the mass of paperwork on his desk. "I've been talking to those idiots at Lowry for half the morning. Bunch of damned hotshots in the Army Air Corps. You'd think I asked for the world instead of one stinking little plane. I'm sick of the army. Sick of the war."

"We all are," Luke said. "It's gone on too long."

"Too many men have died. Good men." He focused on Luke through bloodshot eyes. "How much do you know about this project Fermi is working on?"

The only details Luke had came from Shana. "That information is top secret."

"A bomb," Hughes said. "A powerful bomb that can destroy an entire city. An atomic bomb."

That was exactly what Shana had said. How would she have that knowledge? If she was a spy, she'd know.

Luke immediately rejected that notion. She wasn't a traitor. He'd been wrong about women before, especially about his former fiancée, but he'd seen into Shana's soul. With all his heart, he believed she was a good person.

But how did she know about the bomb? Much as he hated to think about her lunatic claim about time travel, he had to take it under consideration. She might know about Fermi's project because—in her era—the bomb had already been dropped.

"We don't need more bombs," Hughes said. "It's time for all the killing to stop."

Considering that the captain had gunned down an intruder in cold blood, his sentiment lacked sincerity. He thought everybody else should hang up their weapons, but it was okay for him to kill a man and stash his body in a cold, dark shed.

"About the plane," Luke said.

"Tomorrow. We'll have a plane by noon tomorrow. Frankly, I can't wait to get that son of a bitch Fermi off my base."

Waiting until tomorrow created a problem. Shana was supposed to deliver Fermi to the spies tomorrow morning. If she didn't fulfill her end of the bargain, they might make a move on their own. Even worse, they might come after her.

"Sir, I suggest that we double the guards on Fermi until his departure."

"Take care of it." He flapped his hand in a dismissive gesture. "Hey, what happened with the girl? Did she make contact with the Russians while you were in Aspen?"

Luke looked his commanding officer straight in the face and lied. "No, sir. She did not."

His brow lowered in a scowl, and he seemed to be considering Luke's words. Even in his debilitated state, he might be able to recognize a deception. "What are you telling me, Rawlins?"

Luke phrased his statement carefully to

avoid lying. "I didn't observe Shana making contact."

"I still don't trust her," the captain said. "Make sure you don't let that broad out of your sight."

"Yes, sir."

That was an order Luke fully intended to obey.

Chapter Thirteen

Shana's plain bedroom in the main house at Camp Hale offered zero opportunity for vanity. There wasn't even a mirror. Still, she dressed carefully in her new slacks and blouse. After wearing heavy boots, her little black flats felt light as air and feminine. She smoothed the creases in her slacks, wondering how anybody in this era managed to look neat without wrinkle-free fabrics, and she wished for some kind of jewelry to brighten her appearance.

If she'd known before the snowstorm that she was about to time travel, she would have arranged her backpack more carefully—definitely would have brought along a change of underwear. Now she had to make do.

Digging through her pack and the pockets

of her ski jacket, she hoped to find a stray pair of earrings. Cubic zirconia would be nice. In this era, everybody would think they were diamonds. All she found was the collection of rocks she'd picked up before the blizzard—a couple of crystals and the small shard of green trinite.

There was a jaunty tap on her door before Luke stepped inside. When he turned toward her, she was surprised to see him grinning—even more surprised when he embraced her and kissed her on the mouth with a casual intimacy.

"What are you up to?" she asked.

"Something I should have done the minute Fermi arrived." He brought her to the window and opened the blinds. "Look."

Within her field of vision were five armed guards facing the forested area two hundred yards away. Other G.I.'s in their white ski uniforms patrolled on snowshoes closer to the trees. The air of desertion that hung over Camp Hale had been replaced by a parade of activity. She even spotted three men riding homely mules with their long ears sticking straight up. "Mules?"

"Officially, we're a cavalry unit," he said. "Mules handle the terrain better than horses."

"What's all the excitement about?"

"Captain Hughes gave me permission to handle security, and that's what I'm doing. I rousted the troops from their bunks and gave each and every one of those dogfaces an assignment."

"Nice work," she said.

"The way I figure, there are only four spies, and I've got over sixty men at my disposal. That ought to be enough manpower to stop them."

"Why didn't Captain Hughes do this before?"

"He's worn out, just putting in his time and waiting for the war to be over." He paused. His enthusiasm dimmed. "The captain isn't like those guys who can't stop twitching, guys with shell shock. But he's not right in the head."

"Where I come from, we call that post-traumatic stress disorder. It's a clinical diagnosis. Was Hughes in battle?"

"He was wounded in the D-day invasion and sent back home. He hasn't actually been with the 10th for very long, but he's from Colorado and knows how to ski, so he ended up here."

"Where he doesn't really care what's happening."

"That's about the size of it," he said. "I've got to admit that I was feeling the same way myself. Tired to the bone. Sick of dragging myself through a war that seemed like it would go on forever. Hopeless."

"Obviously," she said as she glanced out the window again, "you've gotten your act together."

"Because of you."

When she looked up at him, she saw energy and vitality radiating as bright as a new star. She warmed herself in his heat, glad that she'd been a part of his healing process.

Reaching over to take his hand, she dropped the stones she'd been holding. Luke stooped to pick them up. He turned the glistening trinite to catch the light. "What is this?"

"A rock that I shouldn't have found in Colorado," she said. "I'm hoping Dr. Fermi might have some idea why it was here."

"Let's find out." He leaned close and gave her a little peck on the cheek. "Fermi has been asking to see you."

She followed him through the corridors of the main house to the central conference room with the blackboards. Dr. Fermi and Dr. Douglas—who had asked to be called Dougie—stood at the window, staring out. The instant Fermi saw her, his expression brightened. He rushed toward her and kissed both of her cheeks. The first words out of his mouth were a compliment on her new outfit, and she thanked him. Dr. Fermi knew how to treat a lady.

He turned his attention to business. "Your work on the ore analysis was excellent, Shana. The purity is not as high as I had hoped, but the uranium is—"

"Tuballoy," Dougie reminded. "It's called tuballoy."

"Of course." Dr. Fermi turned back to her. "Now I must ask your expert opinion on which of these three mines will be most useful for our purposes."

Shana was delighted to put her skills to work. This is what she did for a living, analyzing mining probabilities. "We'll need to balance the purity of the tuballoy—" she smiled at Dougie "—with the depth of the vein and prior records of production."

"Technically," Dougie said, "we are only cleared to purchase vanadium so we will also need analysis on that by-product."

"Of course." Dougie's reference to the code name for uranium and the fake purchase of the vanadium alloy reminded her of the need for secrecy surrounding the Manhattan Project. "I hope you gentlemen aren't too disappointed with the results of my geological analysis."

"My true sadness is being under guard," Fermi said as he glanced toward Luke. "While in Colorado, I had hoped to go skiing."

"The snow isn't much good," Luke said. "If we have another warm day, it'll be nothing but mush."

"But I see storm clouds moving in." He pointed toward the window. "We could have another blizzard."

Another blizzard? Shana moved to the window. She'd been preoccupied with watching the activity on the ground and hadn't noticed the dark clouds gathering to the north. The first blizzard had brought her here to 1945. Would a second blizzard return her to her own millennium? It was imperative to find out.

She turned to Dougie whose expression was morose. "This is off the subject, Dougie, but do you remember before when we were talking about time travel?"

"I remember," Dougie said.

Behind her back, she heard Luke clear his throat loudly, reminding her that this topic was taboo. But she had to find out. "You suggested that there might be an emotional or psychological basis for time travel. Something Einstein said."

Though he nodded, his forehead pulled into a frown. "No one can deny the existence of time passing, but the measurement of time in minutes, hours, months and years is created by man."

"So, it's all in the perception," she said.

"Correct," he said. "I perceive, based on visual evidence, that you are here. What if there is a higher sense than vision?"

"An interdimensional perception," she said.

Not being a theoretical physicist, it was difficult to wrap her mind around these concepts. Did time and space really exist? Or were they a construct of man's sensory perception?

She had a much simpler idea. "If our perceptions are based on our sensory evidence, could time and space also be based on emotion?"

"It's possible."

Dr. Dougie went to the blackboard, picked up a piece of chalk and began writing a mathematical formula. His hieroglyphic scribbles made very little sense to Shana. "What are you doing?"

"A perceptual analysis based on the speed of light."

"Too complicated," Fermi said. "Emotion cannot be quantified. We have no measurement for hate or revenge."

Luke stepped forward. "The war could be a measurement. Hundreds of thousands have been killed."

"That is evidence," Fermi said. "But how can it be measured? It has been said that the power of love can move mountains. But where is the quantifiable proof? The facts?

We cannot measure this power in the laboratory."

"Einstein has a theory about the relativity of time and emotion," Dougie said. "Here's the simple explanation. If you touch a hot stove and are burned, time slows down. You see the stove, feel the pain, your body reacts. You may cry out. You may rush to get treatment. Each second seems like an hour."

Shana nodded. "I know exactly what you mean. I was once in a fender bender where I saw the guy who hit my car coming toward me. I knew we'd crash, and everything went into slow motion."

"Compare that intensity to an event without emotional content. Perhaps listening to a boring lecture. The minutes pass like hours."

"So the intensity of the emotion alters my perception of time," she concluded.

She automatically looked toward Luke. When they were together, time flew. Yet, every minute was precious. She would always treasure the images she had of him. His voice would always echo in her ears. "An intense love might be powerful enough to cause time travel."

"Not scientifically," Dougie said.

The science didn't really matter to her. In her heart and her mind, Shana knew that she'd been drawn back through time to be with Luke. He was her destiny, being with him was a stronger need, a stronger perception than fact or mathematical reality.

She wished she could tell Dr. Fermi and his colleague about her own journey through time, wished she could assure him that his own experiment with atomic energy would produce the desired results.

Digging into the pocket of her slacks, she pulled out the small green shard and held it so he could see. "I found this specimen in a mine shaft in this area. It's trinite."

"Very beautiful," Dr. Fermi said.

She knew that trinite had been produced in great quantity after the first test of the atomic bomb in Alamogordo that would take place in a few months' time. The intense heat of the explosion literally created the stone. Fermi would have been there. He would have seen trinite scattered across the earth in shimmering green shards.

"This stone," she said, "isn't found in this

area. Which means that someone must have brought it here."

His eyebrows lifted as though he were expecting a revelation. "It is a most unusual stone."

"I have a feeling that you're going to see a lot of trinite," she said. "And when you do, think of me. And the power of love."

"Bella e brillante," he said. "And also mysterious. What secrets do you hold, Shana Parisi?"

She grinned. "Not as many as you might think."

The most profound explanations were often the simplest. She'd come back in time because of desperately strong, absolutely immeasurable emotions. Because of Luke. He filled the emptiness in her soul and gave her the fantasy she'd always dreamed about but never believed in until now.

He was her time. Her reality. Her destiny.

AFTER THREE HOURS in the conference room listening to Shana and the two scientists discuss geology results, Luke sprawled across the narrow bed in Shana's room and groaned, "It felt like we were locked up in that room for a hundred years."

"Relativity of time and emotion," she said brightly as she went to the window and carefully peeked out. "The less intense the emotion, the slower time passes."

"Right." He wasn't much concerned about her time travel theories. The important thing was that she was here now and she was safe. "I have a theory of my own."

"About time travel?"

"About the Russian spies." He'd done a lot of thinking while being bored this afternoon. "We've already figured out that the Russians had prior knowledge of Fermi's plan to visit Camp Hale. We know that an insider set these wheels in motion. I'm thinking Dr. Dougie might be our traitor."

"Why?"

"He made a stink about being protected."

"So did Dr. Fermi," she pointed out. "Neither one of them likes being sequestered inside."

"What about the other scientist? The one who wasn't around this afternoon."

"Dr. Schultz?" She shook her head. "He's

even more introverted than Dougie. I don't
see him as a spy."

"Somebody on the inside betrayed Fermi."

"They won't get him now," she said firmly.
"You've done everything to keep him safe."

Luke silently congratulated himself. According to hourly reports from guards on duty,
there had been no sign of snipers in the forest.
No disturbance from anywhere in Camp Hale.
The closest they came to excitement this afternoon was when one of the mules took off
after a couple of elk and threw his rider. There
were plenty of yuks about that incident.

Shana was probably right. As long as he
kept security at a high level, Fermi would be
safe until tomorrow when the plane arrived
from Denver to take him back to New
Mexico. And then what would happen? He
wanted to take the rest of the week off.
Before he shipped out, he wanted to spend
every free moment with Shana.

Bella e brilliante. She stood at the edge of
her window where the fading light of dusk
shone gently upon her features. Her stillness
intrigued him. Her natural beauty never
failed to excite him.

It was hard to believe that such a fine woman had taken a shine to him. Though much of her personal history remained a mystery, he could tell that she'd been brought up well. Her training and expertise in geology was obvious. He wouldn't be surprised to find out that she really was the daughter of an ambassador. Someone important. Someone with class.

She brushed a strand of black hair off her forehead. A soft sigh pushed through her full lips. Beautiful! If he didn't leave her bedroom right now, he'd be tempted to make love to her in spite of the lack of privacy. Even though her bedroom was in a separate wing from the others, there were too many G.I.'s running to him with their reports.

"It looks cold out there," she said.

All afternoon, the storm clouds had been thickening. It was winter's last gasp. "I'll keep you warm."

"I like that promise."

Oh man! If he stayed here one more minute, he wouldn't be able to resist her. Luke hauled himself off the bed. "I'm going to tour the perimeter before dinner. Make sure everybody is in their place before nightfall."

"Great idea," she said. "I'll come with you."

"Whoa, there. You can't go outside. You need protection as much as Fermi."

"I'll be okay. At least for today. The bad guys aren't going to hurt me before tomorrow. That's when I'm supposed to deliver Dr. Fermi." She made a twirling motion with her hand. "Turn around and look the other way while I get changed."

It was a little late for modesty. He'd already seen her naked. His intimate knowledge of her body could fill an encyclopedia. "You don't need to change clothes because you're not coming with me."

"I won't get in the way." She started unbuttoning her blouse, revealing the silky skin above her breasts. "I don't like the idea of you parading around in front of the bad guys. Remember, they're after you."

"Maybe."

"There's no maybe about it. They came after us on the pass with guns blazing."

She shot a challenging glance in his direction as she slipped off her blouse. The curve of her shoulders was sheer perfection. Before he had a chance to admire the rest of her sexy body, she thrust her arms into her long-sleeved uniform shirt, and the olive drab swallowed her up. She wiggled out of her trousers and threw on the baggy fatigue pants.

He repeated, "You aren't coming with me."

"It seems to me that dusk is the worst possible time for you to step outside. Everything is gray and shadowy."

He agreed. If he'd been planning an attack, this was the time of day he'd choose. At the end of their watch, the guards were tired. Visibility was poor. "Nighttime won't be much better. That blanket of clouds is going to hide the moonlight. Not to mention that it could start snowing at any minute."

"Where I come from, we have meteorologists who predict the weather."

"We've got weathermen." And it didn't take a scientist to tell him the snow was coming. He could see the threat. He could feel it in his bones.

She brushed past him on the way to the bed where she sat to pull on her socks and boots. "The only way you're going to stop me from coming with you is to stay here. Inside. In safety."

"That's not my job."

"I will not sit back and watch while you put yourself in danger."

"I'm not in danger."

"Really?" Her sarcasm was evident. "I'll bet you're protecting Martin and Henry."

Actually, he was. He'd taken the threat seriously enough to remove Martin and Henry from the regular rotation of guard duty. He'd also moved them from their barracks into the main house. "The boys are safe. They're sacked out right next door to Fermi."

"Aha! That means you acknowledge there's a threat."

"Damn right. That's why I have the entire base on alert."

As he watched her tighten the laces on her boots, his frustration mounted. In the army, the chain of command was crystal clear and there was no disputing your orders. But when a man was dealing with a woman? Hell, he might as well just give up and let her have her way.

She bounced to her feet. "Ready."

"Too bad you changed," he drawled. "I've decided to stay here with you."

Though crestfallen, she gave a brisk nod. "Good choice."

He couldn't keep his hands off her for one more minute. As he reached out for her, he heard noise from the hall. The sounds of a disturbance inside the house.

Duty called. His reaction was immediate. Luke slung his Garand rifle over his shoulder and loosened his handgun from the holster.

He ran down the hall to the right angle corner. The floor plan of the main house was a horseshoe. In the center were the conference rooms and offices. The two wings were bedrooms. The guard who was supposed to be stationed at this juncture was gone from his post. "Damn."

Looking over his shoulder, he realized that Shana was right behind him. "Go back to your room."

"Not without a gun," she said. "I'd be alone in this wing. Unprotected."

He didn't have time to argue with her logic.

A blast of gunfire erupted.

Chapter Fourteen

Staying close to the wall, Shana followed Luke as he made his way cautiously down the center corridor toward the south wing at the opposite side of the main house. Her ears rang with the sounds of battle. Boot heels pounding on wood floors. Door slamming. Shouts of anger and of fear. And gunfire. Oh my God, the gunfire.

In spite of Luke's precautions, the Russians must have gotten past the guards. They had entered the house.

And she was walking toward them. Why? Without a gun or any other weapon, she wouldn't be much help. The only way she could fight back was if she got close enough to use her martial arts skills. These 1945 guys had probably never seen karate before. It might be an advantage.

And she didn't want to stay behind in her room, cowering behind the door. Too easily, she remembered how the Russian had broken in to her hotel room in Aspen and overpowered her.

Halfway down the hall, Luke whipped open the door to the conference room. "In here," he ordered.

She darted inside. The fading light of dusk shone across the table and against the blackboard where Dr. Douglas had tried to explain life and love with a mathematical formula. A new paradigm flashed through her mind: Danger plus threat equals death. She could smell it in the air. Tonight, someone would die.

"Stay in here," Luke whispered. "Find a place to hide."

"What about you?"

"I'll come back for you."

She wished she could believe that promise, but there were no guarantees in war. And this was war. Maybe not the front lines, maybe not the organized battlefront, but they were fighting for their lives.

Luke reacted to a sound she didn't hear.

His rifle raised to his shoulder. "Show your-self."

A man rose from the end of the table. His hands were raised high over his head. "Don't shoot."

Though the shadows, she recognized Dr. Fermi. "What are you doing here?"

He pointed to several notepads and papers strewn across the table. "Working."

Thank God, he was all right. It was a stroke of good fortune that he'd been here rather than in his bedroom when the assault took place.

Luke motioned him forward. In a quiet steady voice, he said, "When I give the word, I want you both to run down the hall to the right. The door to the fire escape is at the end of that wing right beside the latrine. Go down it."

"What about you?" Shana asked.

"I'll be right behind you."

He opened the door a crack, peered outside and quickly closed it again. "Some-body's coming."

He hustled them toward the back of the room and into a closet. Quickly, he closed the door. Inside the small dark space, Shana stood behind Luke's broad back. She rested her palm against his shoulder blade. His strength flowed through her. He was brave and smart; he wouldn't let anything bad happen to her.

From outside the closet door, she heard the heavy thud of boot heels walking across the wood floor.

Dr. Fermi gave her arm a reassuring pat and laced his fingers through her free hand. He should have been even more terrified than she was. The attackers wanted him. He was their target.

Each second dragged more slowly than an hour—proof of the relative perception of time. Shana felt as if her hand was poised above a hot stove, waiting to be burned, waiting to be shot.

The footsteps halted outside the closet. The door handle rattled as it turned.

Luke threw all his weight against the door as he sprang forward and launched himself into a man dressed in army fatigues and helmet. The man staggered backward, off balance.

Luke pressed his advantage. With a swipe of his hand, he disarmed his opponent. Using his own pistol, he unloaded a hard blow to the jaw. The other man crumpled to the floor.

Luke motioned to them. "Let's go before anybody notices this guy is missing."

"How do you know he's not one of ours?"

"I know my men." He yanked the cord loose from the window blinds and used it to tie their attacker's hands behind his back. Another cord trussed his ankles. "Got anything I can use for a gag?"

"Here." Dr. Fermi held out a white handkerchief. "It's been used, but—"

"It's perfect."

Luke secured the gag and picked up his rifle. He grabbed the handgun used by their attacker and gave it to Shana.

The weight of the automatic pistol—a Beretta—boosted her confidence. At least she wasn't helpless.

"Same plan," Luke said.

At the door, he peeked into the hallway, then motioned them forward. Shana stepped out with Dr. Fermi at her side. They ran only a few steps before she heard a shout. "Halt or I shoot."

She stopped and whirled around. Luke stood facing another man dressed as a 10th Mountain Division soldier. He held a machine gun capable of mowing them all down with a single blast. Luke's Garand rifle aimed at his chest.

"Shana," Luke said calmly, "keep going."

"If she takes one step, you are all dead." His voice was almost unaccented, unlike the man who'd come to Shana's room. He nodded toward his weapon. "This is a hair trigger. Even if you shoot me, you will all die."

Shana suspected that he was telling the truth. Otherwise, Luke would have shot him immediately. Instead, they were in a standoff. Luke stood in the middle of the corridor with his legs braced and his rifle at the ready. Motionless as a statue, it didn't even look as if he was breathing. Was he counting the seconds? Waiting for the other man to blink?

Glancing over her shoulder, she calculated the distance to the corner. At least ten steps. She'd never make it without being hit.

"Looks like you win," she said. "What do you want us to do?"

"Lay down your weapons."

Fermi stepped in front of her, protecting her with his own body. "Enough of this," he said coldly. "I am the one you want. I will come peacefully."

"Yes, you come." The machine gun wavered. "If he comes, I will spare you. All of you."

"He's lying," Luke said calmly. "Dr. Fermi, don't take another step."

The man with the machine gun was breathing hard. Under his helmet, his face was flushed. His mouth pulled into a sneer. "I should kill you all. Now."

"But you can't take the chance," Luke said. "You don't want to harm Fermi. A dead scientist won't do you any good."

Shana saw movement behind the Russian's shoulder. It was Private First Class Henry Harrison. In his boxer shorts and a T-shirt, he looked painfully young and thin, but there was nothing childish about the gun in his hand. He aimed and fired three times into the back of the man with the machine gun.

The Russian's hand jerked wildly. As he spun around, he sprayed bullets across the wall. Then he toppled to the floor.

In a few strides, Luke was beside him. He ripped the machine gun free from the twitching hands of the Russian spy. "Get over here, Henry."

He padded toward them in his stocking feet. His skinny chest heaved in and out, laboring with the process of breathing. His eyes were watery, and Shana thought he might be crying.

Luke hustled them around the corner. He clamped his hand around Henry's arm and gave a shake. "What's going on in the south wing?"

"I don't know, sir. I was sleeping, then I heard all this noise. I rolled off my bed and crawled underneath. Then somebody kicked the door open. Martin wasn't in the room. I haven't seen him. He could be dead."

"Calm down, Henry." Luke shook him again. "How many men are in the assault team? How many more?"

His jaw trembled. "Don't know."

His vulnerability tore at Shana's heart. She

gave him a hug, then looked up into his rapidly blinking eyes. "You saved our lives, Henry. You did good."

Luke took a step back. "Dr. Fermi, we need to get you to safety."

"My colleagues," Fermi said. "I will not leave without them."

Luke peeked around the corner to the center corridor, then looked back at them. "I'd like to oblige you, sir. But we can't gamble with your safety."

Shana knew what had to be done. Dr. Fermi must be kept safe at all costs.

"I'll take Dr. Fermi with me," she said. "We'll go down the fire escape and hook up with the men on guard. You go back for the others."

His eyes narrowed as he considered her plan. Then, he nodded. "The three of you, go."

LUKE SLIPPED AROUND the corner and proceeded down the central corridor to the conference room. The man he'd knocked unconscious was awake and thrashing around on the floor. Luke flipped him to his back and tore the gag from his mouth.

"One question," he said. "How many of you are there?"

Dark brown eyes stared up at him, but the face was youthful and frightened, the lips pinched together in a tight white line.

"Aw, hell." Luke placed the cold steel bore of his handgun against the other man's forehead. "If you don't talk to me, you're of no use. Might as well kill you now."

"*Nyet.*" The voice was high-pitched and wavering.

"How many?"

"Four."

With a sharp whack, he rendered the man unconscious again and replaced the gag. Four men. That made sense. There had been four in the Studebaker.

With this man unconscious and another dead in the hallway, they were down to two.

On the south wing, all the doors on both sides were closed. Five on each side. Shots were being fired, but Luke couldn't tell where they were coming from.

In the hallway, there were two soldiers down—two men from Luke's ill-fated command. How the hell had this happened?

He'd stationed ten men in rotating shifts to

guard the interior of this house. Yet, the spies had gotten past the guards outside and slipped in here using the simple pretext of wearing their uniforms.

At the far end of the corridor, Luke spotted Martin and another G.I. in full uniform. He motioned both of them forward.

"Where are they?"

Martin pointed to the third bedroom door from the end. "Holed up in there. They're shooting from the window."

"Using the other two scientists as hostages?"

"Yes, sir. We believe so."

"I want three more men up here. And I want them now."

The G.I. went to do his bidding, and Luke knelt on the floor beside one of the wounded soldiers. He groaned and clutched at his chest where a dark stain spread across his uniform. He needed to be moved before the action took place here.

"Martin, get the medic."

"Yes, sir."

The door on the third bedroom crashed open.

Without a second's hesitation, Luke opened fire. Five bullets. He emptied his clip.

The big man who stood framed in the doorway fell. Three down. One to go.

But Luke's weapon was dry. No more firepower.

He scooted across the floor, grabbed another pistol. Why hadn't the other man appeared?

Holding his weapon in front of him, Luke entered the bedroom. The two colleagues of Dr. Fermi were inside, bound and gagged.

Where was the fourth man?

SHANA LED THE WAY down the wooden fire escape attached to the side of the two-story building. Behind her was Dr. Fermi. Henry, still wearing only his underwear, brought up the rear.

The stairs were rickety and slick with ice. She clung to the guardrail with one hand and held the pistol in the other.

"Careful," she said as much to herself as the others. "Watch your step."

With the heavy storm clouds overhead, it was difficult to see, almost dark.

The wind hurled small bursts of ice crystals against her cheeks, but her mind barely registered the cold. Her heart pumped too furiously, reacting to a general sense of fear. For her own survival. For Dr. Fermi and Henry. And for Luke, especially for Luke. If anything happened to him, she didn't know what she'd do.

At the bottom of the fire escape, she saw a soldier in full battle gear and helmet. She waved to him. "Help us."

He stood, waiting. At least, Dr. Fermi would be safe. He might have to spend the rest of the night locked in a cell with a dozen armed guards standing around him, but he'd be secure.

She descended the final step and looked into the face of the waiting soldier. It was the Russian who broke into her hotel room. "You."

His sneer was cold, disdainful. "As you promised, you have delivered Fermi to me."

She hadn't come this far to fail. When he caught hold of her wrist holding the gun, she remembered her hours of martial arts training.

Using his own force and weight against him, Shana flung him against the side of the building. Before he could turn, she kicked hard into the center of his back.

He whirled to face her. She unleashed a sharp chop to his gun hand. He dropped the weapon. Another kick to his midsection. He doubled over.

It felt as if she was moving in a dream. Reacting without conscious thought. She had the Russian on the ground, facedown in the snow.

She picked up his pistol and pressed it into the center of his back. "Don't move."

"You betrayed me," he growled. "This is not over."

"For you, it is."

When she looked up, she saw Fermi and Henry staring at her with wide eyes. At the top of the fire escape staircase, Luke appeared.

He was safe. Everything was going to be all right.

Chapter Fifteen

Cruising on an adrenaline high, Shana tried to ignore the rapid flutter of her heart. Though all her senses were on superalert, it was difficult to concentrate. Events were happening too quickly.

She watched as Luke took command of the situation. His orders were concise, and his men rushed to obey. They handcuffed the Russian spy. Before he was dragged off to the guardhouse, he turned toward her and gave her one last evil glare. His hatred rushed at her like a blast of hot wind in the snowy night.

Luke directed her, Dr. Fermi and Henry back up the rickety staircase leading into the main house. When the exit door on the second floor closed behind them, he asked, "What happened?"

Though Henry was shivering so hard that she thought his teeth might fall out, he wasn't at a loss for words. "You should have seen what Shana did. It was sweet. She disarmed that Russian as pretty as you please. Then she kicked him in the back and she knocked him over." His arms were flailing. "Her hands were moving so fast they were a blur. Oh man, it was sweet."

Luke cast a somewhat disbelieving glance in her direction. "You disarmed the Russian?"

She nodded. It had all happened so fast. If she actually stopped to think about what she'd done, she might dissolve into a trembling mass of fear—a delayed but sensible reaction to the fact that she'd used her scant knowledge of karate to attack a very dangerous opponent.

Dr. Fermi said, "Shana has saved our lives. She is a wonder."

"A tigress," Luke said. The briefest hint of a smile touched his mouth. In a quiet voice that only she could hear, he added, "You're my little tigress."

With her level of excitement still running

high, she wanted to claim her prize for being so ferocious. She wanted to leap into his arms, to kiss him until her lips were raw. She wanted to make love. Unfortunately, the night was still young.

"Follow me," Luke said.

He strode down the hall to the corner, turned and kept moving. The body of the spy who had threatened them with a machine gun lay sprawled against the wall. Dead and motionless.

Her stomach clenched. This was the first time Shana had witnessed violent death, and it sobered her. "Were any of the soldiers injured?"

"Two," Luke said. "I want to get over to the infirmary and see if I can help."

"Excuse me," Dr. Fermi cut in. "Dr. Schultz might be of some assistance. Before he studied physics, he was a surgeon."

"That's what we need," Luke said. "The boys were shot up pretty bad."

They rounded the final corner and confronted the aftermath of the main battle. The wood floor was slick with blood. The air smelled like the inside of a gun barrel.

The horror of what had happened sank into Shana's consciousness, and the knot in her stomach tightened. She wanted to get away from here, to wake up from this nightmare and find Luke beside her, comforting her.

Careful not to step through any of the crimson puddles, she moved to a position against the wall and waited quietly while Luke organized his men. She closed her eyes.

HER FIELD OF VISION narrowed. A blurry form took shape beside her. She recognized the young boy with dark eyes and a curly mop of dark hair. When he took her limp hand, she tried to squeeze his fingers. He squeezed back. He had the smile of an angel.

She tried to say his name. "Roberto." But her lips wouldn't move.

He stroked her forehead and said, "Bella e brillante."

Beautiful and smart? She didn't feel wise. Her brain wasn't working properly. Not at all.

"SHANA," LUKE SAID. "Let's go."

Obediently, she plodded along behind

him. Dr. Schultz accompanied them as they left the main house and followed the shoveled pathways toward the infirmary.

Though she didn't remember putting on her outer jacket, she was glad to be wearing it. The night wind whipped around her. Snow fell in quick bursts.

She thought of the beautiful little orphan boy, Roberto. Why had he stepped into her mind? What did it mean? She wanted to believe she was seeing the future when she would finally meet this child who had touched Luke's heart. If they could all be together as a family, life would be truly wonderful.

In the infirmary building, Shana took a seat in the outer waiting room beside a scarred wooden desk. There was nothing she could do but stay out of the way. Luke and Dr. Schultz washed up, then donned surgical masks and gowns. They disappeared into a room that she hoped was more sterile than this outer area where stacks of paperwork waited to be tucked away in the file cabinets.

She leaned her head back and closed her eyes, hoping to return to her vision of

Roberto. But she saw nothing, heard nothing unusual. Once when she fell into this disembodied trance state, she'd heard Beethoven. Another time, there were soft, pink rose petals.

Luke returned to her side. In his white surgical mask and gown, he looked very much like a doctor.

"How are they?" she asked.

"It would have been a lot worse if they hadn't been wearing flak jackets. One of them is in bad shape. Lucky for us that Dr. Schultz knows his stuff." He pulled off his mask. "Do you know anything about giving injections?"

"No." And she was not about to take a crash course in medical procedure. "Why?"

"They need more transfusions," he said as he stood. "And I'm a universal donor."

She remembered reading his dog tag on their first night together. He was P for Protestant, and his blood type was O negative. "Surely, you're not intending to open a vein?"

"Don't make it sound so dramatic. This is a simple procedure."

Maybe for him. She'd only given blood twice in her life. Both times, she'd nearly passed out. There was something peculiar and awful about watching your own blood drain through a tube.

She followed him into an examination room with a cot and a lot of medical equipment arrayed carelessly on the countertop. He gathered the necessary supplies quickly. "I've done this before."

"Half the blood we have on hand is from me. Usually, there's somebody else to stick in the needle, but I can do it myself."

He rolled up his sleeve revealing his muscular wrist and forearm. One-handed, he tied off his upper arm with rubber tubing and swabbed the inside of his elbow. "Once I find the vein, I want you to use tape to secure the needle. Can you do that?"

"I'll try," she said gamely. Shana had just watched a man die. She'd waded through pooling blood on the hardwood floor in the main house. Surely, she could avoid being squeamish about a needle. "You'll have to tell me how to do this."

He sat on the edge of the cot with the

catheter needle poised above his arm. Slowly and deliberately, he inserted the needle into a vein. He didn't flinch.

For Shana, this moment defined Luke's heroism more than when he had a gun in his hand. He was a healer, willing to give himself to save one of his men.

Within seconds, his blood flowed through the catheter into the plastic IV bag.

"Tape it here," he said. "Be careful not to dislodge the needle."

Though her hands were shaky, she managed it. "You should lie down now."

He stretched out on the cot. The mud from his boots smeared across the white sheets. "When that bag is full, I'll tell you how to replace it with another."

"How much blood are you intending to take?"

"Usually it's only a pint," he said. "Right now, we need two."

"Is that safe?"

"The human body has about six quarts of blood. I'll only be losing one."

She pulled up a chair to sit beside him. Her fingers laced through his free hand, and she gently stroked the area above his wrist. The crisp hair on his arm was darker than the sandy brown hair that fell across his forehead. She knew the secrets of his body so very well. The allowing pattern of hair on his chest. The scars on his upper chest and shoulder where he'd been shot. Every feature was branded into her memory.

Her memories shattered when Captain Hughes lurched into the room. His eyes were red, as if he hadn't slept for days. He smelled like old sweat and something else. Liquor?

"Well, Rawlins," he snarled, "your plans to guard Fermi didn't exactly work, did they? I've got two dead spies to explain. And two seriously wounded soldiers."

Luke exhaled a sigh. "No sir, my plan wasn't a success."

Even though Captain Hughes was obviously on his last legs, she wouldn't allow him to march in here with accusations. Shana piped up, "It could have been a hell of a lot worse."

The captain swung his head and focused on her. "How so, Miss Parisi?"

"If Dr. Fermi had been in his room instead

of down the hall in the conference room, the Russians might have grabbed him and gotten away clean." Her tone was calm and rational. "If the wounded soldiers hadn't been wearing flak jackets, they might be dead right now."

"There's another way we're lucky," Luke said. "Dr. Schultz is a surgeon."

"Strange definition of luck," Hughes muttered. "You know there's going to be an official inquiry into this incident."

"Investigation is needed." Though Luke lay flat on his back, his voice was assertive. "In fact, we need an immediate investigation."

"Why? All the spies are in custody."

"As I told you before, someone on the inside gave information to the Russians, telling them Fermi was here. I know this because the spies arrived in Aspen before Fermi arrived on base. They anticipated his trip here."

"His visit to Camp Hale was top secret. Are you saying we have a leak?"

"Yes." Luke watched the plastic tubing carrying his blood to the bag, willing that fluid to move faster. The wounded men needed transfusions.

"That bears looking into," Hughes said. "If someone in the chain of top secret information talked to the spies, the army needs to know."

"The traitor could be closer to home." Luke didn't want to make this accusation because it meant someone at Camp Hale was working with the enemy. He didn't want to believe that one of his men was a traitor. "Someone helped the spies get our uniforms."

"Blame yourself for that breach," the captain said. "You had every man working guard duty on the main house. It was easy for the Russians to slip inside the supply room and procure extra uniforms."

"Is that how it happened?" Shana asked.

"The supply room was broken into," Hughes said, "and the uniforms came from there."

"But nobody actually *saw* the break-in. Nobody *saw* the Russians within the boundaries of Camp Hale," she pointed out. "With everyone on high alert, how could they approach? They would have been noticed."

"What are you suggesting?"

"That the Russians paid someone to bring the uniforms to them."

"None of my men are traitors," he coldly informed her. "This SNAFU was a direct result of too many men going in too many different directions."

"Oh, please," she said. "That explanation sucks."

"Excuse me?"

"If Luke hadn't placed all those men on guard duty, Fermi would be gone right now. You'd have a much bigger problem to explain."

Luke groaned inwardly. Obviously, Shana had no concept of proper respect.

She continued, "Luke did everything right. And you've got two foreign spies in your custody. They just might have intelligence useful to our country. You should be thanking Luke. Instead of reprimanding him, you should give this man a medal."

Hughes looked down his nose at her. "Exactly how many medals does our hero need?"

"You tell me." She stood to confront him.

"I've heard that you served in the D-day invasion. You know the worst horror of war. Fermi's atomic bomb could help bring an end to this slaughter."

"A bigger bomb to end a war." He gave a mirthless laugh. "Hell of a concept, Miss Parisi."

"Would you rather have Fermi's experiments in Russian hands?"

"I've heard enough." The captain raised a hand to his temple. His fingertips massaged at the edge of his hairline. "Sergeant Rawlins, we'll discuss this later. As of now, you're no longer in command."

He turned on his heel and stalked from the room. Luke listened as the sound of his footsteps receded down the corridor. The outer door slammed.

"Sorry if I made things worse," Shana said. "I couldn't sit here and listen to that slacker captain give you a hard time."

"You did good." Not only was she beautiful and smart but also eloquent. She'd defended him better than he could defend himself. "I think you missed your calling. You could have been a damn good lawyer."

"But I hate arguing. I like for everything to be calm, rational and peaceful."

"That's not likely to happen."

He had a nasty feeling that Shana's assessment was correct: there was a traitor at Camp Hale. A traitor who provided the uniforms used by the Russians. Fermi wasn't safe. Not yet.

Earlier, Luke had suspected Dr. Douglas of being involved with the spies. Douglas was intelligent enough to be a mastermind. Plus, Fermi trusted him. But would Douglas allow himself to be captured, trussed up and helpless? Plus, Dr. Douglas and Dr. Schultz had both been under guard. They couldn't have taken the stolen uniforms to the Russians—not unless they were working with someone else, someone who could easily approach the supply room.

Luke had to face the painful truth. The traitor was one of his own men. Whoever it was, he'd sold out Fermi and Luke and his country. For what? Probably money. A reward for turning over the genius who had invented a bomb powerful enough to destroy a city could be astronomical. If somebody like Martin had been offered a big payoff, he might be tempted.

Though Luke had been formally relieved of his command position, he wasn't done protecting Fermi.

Shana approached him with an army blanket she'd found in a storage closet by the door. Tenderly, she tucked it around him.

"I'm not cold," he said.

"Of course you are. I'm cold so you must be."

This feminine logic—no matter how mis-guided—was unstoppable. Luke didn't bother to argue.

"It's strange," she said. "When I was on the staircase with Fermi and Henry, it was almost snowing. But I didn't feel cold at all."

"That's a battle response. Your body is so focused on action, that you don't feel much of anything." When he looked up at her delicate features, he found it difficult to believe that this lady could take out an armed Russian spy. "How'd you disarm him, ti-gress?"

"Karate," she said. "It's a type of fighting that everybody is going to know about in the future. My company made me take classes before I was stationed in Kuwait."

"Why?"

"Terrorists," she said. "Those are the enemies in my era, and they don't hesitate to attack civilians. When I was working in an area where they were active, I needed to be prepared to defend myself. It's weird that I never used that training until now."

"Henry can't stop talking about it. He thinks you're pretty doggone amazing."

Lowering her face near his, she whispered, "And what do you think?"

"I *know* you're amazing."

Her soft lips joined with his, and a gentle warmth spread through his body. He wanted to be with her tonight, to peel away her baggy fatigues and revel in her sweet, sexy arms. Unfortunately, that wasn't a realistic possibility. After tonight, the entire base was focused on Shana and her karate skills. They had no privacy.

She pulled away from him. "What do we do next?"

"Make love." He felt his lips curve in a grin. The loss of blood was making him a little loopy.

"I'd like that." She caressed his forehead.

"I wish we could make love. Now. And later. All night."

As his blood drained through the IV, Luke knew he was weakening. Concentration took an effort. "But we need to make sure Fermi is safe."

"There must be enough guards," she said. "Even Captain Hughes couldn't mess that up."

She was probably right. Tonight, with the Russians locked up in the guardhouse, Fermi would be well-protected, even if there was a traitor at Camp Hale. Nobody would dare make a move tonight with the men on high alert. "What about tomorrow?" he murmured.

"The plane is supposed to arrive at noon," she said. "We tuck Fermi and his two buddies inside, and that's that. They're on their way back to New Mexico."

"Unless the snow picks up."

Not even the hotshot fighter pilots from the Army Air Corps would attempt a landing in blizzard conditions. Safe evacuation by aircraft should be treated as a remote possibility. Luke needed a backup plan.

Tonight, he'd make a phone call to Jack

Swenson—world-class skier and expert marksman. Jack could be trusted. He'd pick up Fermi first thing tomorrow morning and drive away from Camp Hale before the traitor knew what hit him.

Satisfied with that solution, Luke turned his attention to another pressing issue. Shana's safety. She'd betrayed the Russian; that action might make her a target for revenge.

He glanced toward the IV bag on the pole. Almost full. "When we're done here, I want to take you to the cabin."

"Just the two of us?"

He nodded. "I don't want to spend the entire night worrying about whether or not the traitor will come after you."

He had another reason for returning to the cabin. His photograph of Roberto was missing from his wallet, and the last time he remembered seeing it was at the cabin. That picture represented the most important reason he continued to fight. The most important? Not anymore.

Shana was his reason for living. She gave him a glimpse into the future—a future that included her as part of his life.

Chapter Sixteen

At ten minutes past ten o'clock, Luke nodded to the armed guard who was posted outside Shana's room. "Good evening, Henry."

The skinny private who had grown up a lot in the past few days gave him a grin. "Good evening, sir."

"Do you remember what we talked about earlier?"

"You bet your bottom dollar." He winked as he checked his wristwatch. "I was just about to take a little break. Maybe fifteen minutes or so."

"Thanks, Henry."

That fifteen minutes would give Luke enough time to make his getaway with Shana. The best way to protect her from the traitorous threat at Camp Hale was to leave. They'd be safe at the cabin.

He paused with his hand on the doorknob, aware of another factor that was driving him—an indefinable urgency. He was *supposed* to take her to the cabin tonight. It was their fate, their destiny.

Why? He didn't know.

What did he expect to happen? That, too, was a mystery.

But he was one hundred percent certain that they had to be at the cabin. It was the first step in an inevitable chain of events that *must* happen.

He slipped into her room. She'd shed her baggy olive-drab fatigues and dressed in the fitted ski pants, turtleneck and boots she'd worn the first time he saw her. Her twenty-first century clothing?

She rushed into his arms and hugged him tightly. "Luke, do we have to go tonight? It's cold out there."

"I know."

"We can stay here and barricade the door. The Russians are locked up in the guard-house. We ought to be safe tonight."

The thought of staying here and lying beside her on the bed was pretty damned seductive. After giving two pints of blood, he was exhausted. It'd be heaven to just lie here and close his eyes. But he couldn't do that, couldn't ignore the urge that was driving him. "I can't explain it, but I have an instinct. We need to be at the cabin tonight. We're supposed to be there."

She studied his face for a moment, then solemnly nodded. "I trust your instincts. Let's move."

They gathered up her skis. At the end of the corridor, they exited outside. The looming blizzard hadn't yet struck, but the skies were dark and cloudy. No moon tonight.

In minutes, they descended the staircase to the spot where he'd left his own cross-country skis, all waxed and ready to go. With his skis on his shoulder, he led her past the mess hall and the infirmary where the two wounded men were doing well and were expected to recover. Beyond the last of the barracks, the pathways were no longer cleared.

They fastened their skis into their bindings and set out across the open terrain that led to the forests where the snipers had been hiding. A heavy wind coiled around him. Brittle crystals of snow stung his cheeks.

Squinting, he peered into the thick wall of trees where the sniper had been hiding. The threat from the Russians was over, but he couldn't shake his wariness. Someone was watching.

Someone in Camp Hale was a traitor, dangerous and vengeful. Luke turned and looked over his shoulder. Shana was struggling to keep up with him. Behind her, he saw only the shadows from the camp. There was no sign that anyone was following. Even if they came later, the wind and the light snow would cover the tracks from their skis. He and Shana would be able to disappear tonight. They'd be safe.

Breathing hard, she stopped behind him. "Skiing in the dark is hard. I can't see all the little bumps and ridges."

"Once we get into the forest, we'll be able to take off our skis. There's only a couple of inches of snow left between the trees."

"Good," she said with a gasp.

"Then we can hike. Uphill."

"Swell," she muttered. "Are you trying to kill me?"

It was the opposite. He'd gladly lay down his life to keep her safe. Digging in with his poles, he went forward.

This route to his cabin was longer than the other way, but the hills weren't so steep and they were farther from the service roads and the normal activity of Camp Hale.

By the time they reached the final approach through the trees, his mind had gone numb. Without conscious thought, his physical training directed his movements. His heartbeat synchronized with the forward motion of his skis. Left, then right, then left. He stopped and waited for Shana to catch up.

"We're almost there," he assured her.

"Hooray," she said weakly.

A sliver of moonlight cut through the clouds and shone upon her. Her face was pink from exertion and cold. Her dark eyes glittered. She was a far different woman from the wounded little bird he'd rescued on the slopes when they first met. Shana could handle anything life threw at her; she was the strongest woman he'd ever known. "Have I told you how beautiful you are?"

"Don't start," she warned. "All I'm thinking about right now is getting inside that cabin and lighting up a fire in the potbellied stove."

The last hike through the trees was steadily uphill but not difficult. Luke shoved open the door to the cabin and pulled her inside. Simultaneously, they dropped their skis on the floor and collapsed across the narrow cot.

The last time Luke had been here, he'd been looking forward to drinking whiskey until he passed out and forgot all his sorrows. He'd been depressed, emotionally wounded by the war. If death had caught up with him at that moment, he wouldn't have minded too much.

Then Shana tumbled into his lonely life. Tromping willy-nilly through all his preconceived ideas, she infuriated him and excited him at the same time. She'd taught him how to laugh. Because of her, he'd found the courage to step forward and be a leader. Because of her, he was a man again.

"I'm starving," she said. "I could even eat one of those disgusting K rations."

Luke dragged himself off the bed and fetched one of the cardboard boxes of K rations, which he placed on the bed beside her. Then he went to the potbellied stove and laid a fire from the kindling in the wood box. He lit a few of the lanterns.

If anyone came searching for them, the smoke from the chimney would give away their location. But the alternative was to freeze to death. He latched the cabin door and placed his handgun on the table within easy reach.

At the table, he picked up the photograph of Roberto. Looking at the picture always made him grin. In only a few days, Luke would return to Italy. "I'm going to find him. If it's the last thing I do, I'm going to make sure Roberto has a chance at a good life."

"I'm coming with you," Shana announced with a flourish of the candy bar from the K ration box.

"To Italy? To the front lines of the war?"

"The alternative is to let you go by yourself. Maybe to never see you again. That's not going to happen, Luke. I'll find a way to get overseas."

He picked up a thin piece of paper from the table. "What's this?"

Shana leaned forward to see what he was holding, then she made a grab for the paper. "It's nothing."

"Looks like a receipt from a hotel." He turned it over. On the back, she'd scribbled a note. He read aloud. "Thanks for saving my life. Going to town. Goodbye forever, Shana."

She groaned. "A little dramatic, huh? But I was mad at you when I wrote that. You abandoned me here."

Freely, he admitted, "I was a jerk."

He'd been so caught up in his own needs, his own lousy depression, that he didn't realize the magnitude of the gift she'd given him. Her trust. Her affection. A fantasy.

As he gazed at her in the soft glow from the lanterns, Luke appreciated her outward beauty. Her thick, shiny, black hair. The sexy shimmer of her eyes. And those lips, those kissable lips. Looking at her made him warmer than the heat that radiated from the potbellied stove.

Even more, he liked who she was inside—curious and clever and loyal and brainy.

He flipped over the hotel receipt. "The Leadville Lodgings. Never heard of it."

"Probably didn't exist in 1945," she said with a shrug. "You've got to expect a few changes in the past sixty or so years."

Ever since she'd told him that she'd come from the future, she stuck tight to that story. All her other ruses had been brushed aside. The amnesia. The claim that everybody she knew was in Kuwait. Her steadfast adherence to that story almost convinced him that she'd actually traveled through time.

Glancing down, he read the date confirming her hotel reservation. The year was 2006. "Son of a bitch."

Stunned, he stared at the slip of paper. 2006? The next millennium? "This reservation says you're staying at the Leadville Lodgings for four days, starting on May 6, 2006."

"Of course." As she nibbled at the K ration food substitute, her nose wrinkled in disgust. "That's when I made the reservation. Haven't you been listening to me? I told you that I came back in time."

"But this is proof."

She might have fabricated this receipt. But if she had, why wouldn't she have mentioned it before? This was the truth, printed in black and white. "You really are from the future."

"Not anymore." She stepped off the bed and into his arms. "This is where I belong."

He kissed her hard, needing to assure himself that this miracle was true. She was really here. With him. "So it's not goodbye forever."

"Hello." She reached up. With her fingertip, she touched the tip of his nose. "Hello forever, Luke."

They were meant to be together. Neither time nor distance could keep them apart.

THE NARROW COT in the cabin was just large enough for them to lie cradled in each other's arms, but Shana didn't mind a bit. Being pressed tightly against Luke's naked body felt like the most comfortable place on the planet.

She remembered her first night in this small, rustic cabin. That night had been a fantasy. They'd been two strangers thrown together by the storm.

Tonight was real. Very real. She knew the feel of his hard, muscular chest against her body. She knew the taste of his lips, the scent of his body.

His intense blue eyes gazed steadily into hers. No longer searching for answers, he accepted her.

When he eased her onto her back and rose above her, she gladly allowed him to dominate her in every way. His teasing fingers pinched her taut nipples, sending a current of sensation racing through her. His mouth ravaged hers, leaving her gasping. When he penetrated her, the explosion of pleasure lifted her out of herself. She was soaring on another plane of existence. Echoes from this different place called to her. Purposely, she silenced them. She would never leave Luke. Never.

For long moments, he stayed inside her. Joined. Waiting.

"This is what I want," she whispered. "For all eternity."

"I want you to be with me forever." His voice rumbled inside his chest. "Marry me."

Without the slightest hesitation, she replied, "Yes."

A devilish grin touched the corners of his mouth. With one last kiss, he separated from her and left the bed. In the light from the lanterns, his naked body was magnificent. Absolutely perfect. He picked up his trousers from the floor and rummaged through the pockets.

"I want to do this right," he said. "But I don't have a diamond. This ring will have to do."

He returned to the side of the bed and went down on one knee. In his hand, he held a silver ring with the 10th Mountain Division insignia of crossed swords.

Luke cleared his throat. "Will you be my wife?"

"I already said yes."

"This is more formal. A binding contract that will never be broken."

She held his hand with both of hers. "You can ask me a thousand times, and my answer will always be the same."

When he slipped the ring on her engagement finger, it was too loose. She moved it to the middle finger. "It almost fits."

"For me, it's a pinkie ring."

She leaned forward and kissed him. "I should give you something, too."

"Lady, you've given me more than you know."

She scrambled out from under the covers and found her backpack. Digging around inside, she found the small shard of green trinite. "This," she said. "Someday, we'll have it made into a ring."

His fingers closed around the stone. "I'll keep it with me. Always."

In spite of the heat generated by the pot-bellied stove, the interior of the cabin was chilly, and they both slipped under the covers. Lying in each other's arms, they fell asleep.

THE NEXT MORNING, she awoke to the scent of coffee and déjà vu. Sunlight slanted through the window. The air held a definite chill. Luke was already up and dressed, feeding wood into the stove. This was almost exactly like the last time she'd awakened in this cabin.

Shana bolted upright on the bed. "You're not leaving me," she said firmly.

Instead of grumbling and charging out the door, Luke came toward her and sat on the edge of the bed. His features relaxed into a companionable smile as he took her hand and kissed her fingers just above his 10th Mountain Division ring.

The realization struck her. They were engaged!

"Why are you dressed?" she asked.

"It's going to be a busy morning."

Somehow, she'd had the impression that they were going to spend most of their time together, hopefully, in bed. "Why? What's going on?"

"I guess I never explained my plans for Fermi."

Worried that he was about to plunge them into trouble again, she pulled her hand away. "You haven't explained anything."

"The weather's bad," he said. "A blizzard could hit at any minute. So I don't expect any aircraft landing at Camp Hale today."

She nodded. This much she understood. "And so?"

"Last night I put in a telephone call to Jack Swenson. He's going to meet me at Camp

Hale early this morning. We'll load Fermi and his two colleagues into Jack's station wagon, and he can drive away safely."

"That seems unnecessarily complicated. Why should Jack be involved?"

"Because I trust him," Luke said. "Anybody at Camp Hale could be a traitor, and I'm sure as hell not going to trust Fermi to someone who might kidnap him."

Blinking to clear away the last dregs of sleep, she considered his plan from a couple of different angles. It seemed to make sense. "Are you sure you can trust Jack?"

"With my life."

She tugged on his sleeve and pulled him closer for a warm embrace. Though she would have preferred unbuttoning his shirt and dragging him back into bed, she understood. Fermi's safety came first.

"I'll be dressed in a minute," she said.

"No rush." He twirled a strand of her hair between his fingers before tucking it behind her ear. "I'd rather have you stay where you'll be safe."

After last night's trek though the snow, a lazy morning in bed sounded wonderful. But her adrenaline was already pumping. Even without caffeine, she was wide-awake, alert to danger.

An annoying little doubt pushed to the front of her mind. "As long as the Russians stay locked up, I'm not in danger. Not as much as you. Or Henry or Martin for that matter."

"Henry and Martin? Why do you think they're in danger?"

"Remember, I told you. When the Russian spy came into my room in Aspen, he said you and Henry and Martin needed to be eliminated. That's why he chased after us on Independence Pass."

Luke went to the potbellied stove and removed the coffeepot. He poured her a mug. "That had to be to avenge the murder of the other spy, the one Captain Hughes shot."

"Murder?" This was the first she'd heard about a murder. "The captain killed somebody?"

"There was a fifth Russian. He was sneaking around in the files on the captain's desk."

She vaguely recalled Luke mentioning a hypothetical situation about why someone would want to snoop through the papers on the captain's desk. "What happened to this spy?"

"Hughes shot him dead. Then he ordered me and Martin and Henry to stash the body in a storage shed."

"To cover up what he'd done." She took the coffee mug from Luke's hand and took a gulp. The picture in her mind became clear. "Oh my God. It's a cover-up."

"What are you talking about?"

"In my millennium, we're a lot more cynical. We know that politicians and top officials sometimes lie, and we sure as hell know about cover-ups."

"You're saying that the captain wanted to hide the murder." Luke shrugged. "I can believe that."

"The only way he could cover up the murder was to eliminate the witnesses. You, Henry and Martin. That's why the Russians came after us. Because Captain Hughes told them to."

"If he was working with them, why shoot one of them?"

"A falling-out among traitors," she said darkly. "Captain Hughes is your traitor, Luke. He knew the top secret information about Dr. Fermi's visit. He hates and resents the army. And Dr. Fermi, too."

She set down her coffee, climbed out of bed and began pulling on her clothes. No way would she let Luke walk back into Camp Hale where Hughes was waiting like a black widow spider in the middle of his web.

"What are you doing?" he asked.

"I'm coming with you."

"Shana, no." He held her shoulders. "This will all go smoothly. Everything is going to be fine. There's no reason for you to be in danger."

"You're my reason," she said. "If anything happened to you—"

"It won't."

Before she could raise a logical objection, he slipped into his parka and opened the door. Outside the cabin, it was icy cold. Snowflakes danced on the wind.

"Please, Luke. Don't go."

"I'll be back before you know it," he promised. "Trust me, Shana. Whether it's 1945 or sixty years later, we're meant to be together. You and me? We'll have our happily ever after."

As he closed the door behind himself, she threw on her boots and her parka. An unreasonable sense of panic churned through her causing her fingers to tremble as she grabbed her skis.

Something terrible was about to happen. She could feel it. Desperately, she wished she could have the same blind faith that Luke had. The trust. The belief that everything would turn out all right.

When she opened the cabin door, he was already gone. All that was left of him were footprints in the snow.

Chapter Seventeen

Trying to catch up to Luke was futile. He was in peak condition, and Shana was only in average shape. Still, she exerted every effort as she followed his footprints. He'd hiked uphill through the trees.

She remembered enough of her surroundings to guess that he had taken the steep route back to Camp Hale. Gasping, she struggled to pull enough oxygen into her lungs.

At the edge of the forest, she confronted a wide-open expanse of snow. Dark storm clouds loomed overhead. The wind kicked up whirling gusts of snow. The trail of Luke's skis across the ridge was fading. He was almost erased.

She clicked her skis into the bindings and

charged into the impending blizzard. Her arms and legs churned as she skied against the wind, straining at the edge of her physical endurance. Finally, she reached the point where she had stood once before—the place where she first saw Camp Hale.

It was gone! The barracks, the main house, the barns and all the G.I.'s had vanished. She squeezed her eyelids closed.

SHE LAY IN A HOSPITAL bed, staring up at a cream-colored ceiling. A CD player beside her resonated with classical music. The view from the windows was a pristine mountain on a clear day.

This was all wrong. All wrong.

She had to get away from here. Back to Luke. He needed her.

She struggled under the thin blanket that covered her. But her arms and legs wouldn't move. She was paralyzed. Helpless.

HER EYES OPENED, and she saw the army camp. It was there. *Real.* At the base of this rugged slope, a couple of hundred yards away, she saw Luke at the edge of the road.

He was talking to someone who stood beside an old station wagon. Jack Swenson?

"Luke!" She screamed his name, but the wind swallowed her words.

Her skis aimed downhill, and she moved as quickly as possible. The worst thing that could happen now would be if she fell. Her skis skidded across a patch of ice, but she managed to stay on her feet.

Pausing to catch her breath, she saw others joining Luke beside the car. It was Dr. Fermi and the other two scientists.

Maybe Luke was right. Maybe Dr. Fermi's escape would take place without a hitch. She prayed that was true, prayed that her race against time was unnecessary.

She was only twenty yards away when she saw the station wagon pull away. Dr. Fermi was safely on his way back to New Mexico where he could complete his research. History remained intact.

Luke spotted her. When he waved, the snow swirled around him. In moments, the full force of the blizzard would hit.

Then she saw the threat. Two men emerged from the buildings of Camp Hale.

Both were dressed in the all-white ski uniform with the hoods of their parkas pulled up, but she knew who they were. Captain Hughes and the Russian.

"Luke," she called out to him. "Behind you."

He turned. In a well-practiced motion, he slung his Garand rifle over his shoulder, dropped to one knee and took aim.

One of the men approaching did the same.

Luke fired first. The blast echoed against the slopes. The man with the rifle went down.

The other held a handgun. His arm thrust out straight in front of him. He got off two shots before Luke took him down.

Both of the skiers who tried to attack Luke were on the ground. The red of their blood contrasted with the blanket of snow.

Relief overwhelmed her. The threat was gone, and Luke was safe. She'd been worried for no reason. They had their whole future ahead of them. They'd be married and live happily ever after.

Luke lowered his arms. The rifle fell from his gloved hands. When he rose to his feet, he staggered. His knees gave out and he crumpled to the ground.

Frantically, she skied toward him. When she reached his body, she kicked off her skis and knelt beside him, cradling his upper body against her breasts. There was blood on his white parka. It seemed to come mostly from his left arm.

His shimmering blue eyes gazed up at her. "You were right," he said. "That was Captain Hughes and the Russian. Hughes must have released that bastard from the guardhouse."

She didn't give a damn about being right. "Stay with me. You're going to be all right."

"I'm going to be with you, Shana." His right arm reached toward her, then fell limply into the snow. "I love you."

"I love you, too."

His eyelids fluttered closed. He wasn't dead yet. She could feel his strong heart beating. He couldn't die. Not Luke. Not the only man she'd ever loved. Fate would not be that cruel.

Frantically, she screamed, "Help us. Somebody help us."

Hadn't anyone else heard the gunfire? Where were the rest of the G.I.'s at the camp?

The snowfall started suddenly. A curtain of white surrounded her. Though she clung fiercely to Luke, her body felt disconnected. The inside of her head went into a dizzying spin. When she looked up, a glowing circle of light descended through the clouds and the snow, and she knew that she would be pulled into that vortex.

She was being lifted, torn away from Luke. Her heart shattered as she fell into the depths of despair.

SHANA BOLTED UPRIGHT in the hospital bed. This was the same place she'd dreamed about. Pink roses in a vase. A CD playing Beethoven.

This was all wrong. She had to get out of here, had to find Luke.

As she reached toward the IV positioned in her arm, a young boy with a curly mop of dark hair placed his hand over the needle. He had the eyes of an angel.

"Are you really awake this time?" he asked.

"I'm awake," she said more harshly than she'd intended. "Who are you?"

"Roberto."

Luke's Roberto? If he was here, then Luke couldn't be far away. "Where is he?"

"You should quiet down." His eyebrows pulled into a scowl. "You've been very, very sick."

An elderly doctor in a white lab coat entered the room. Though he had to be in his seventies, he was an undeniably handsome man. "Welcome, Shana. I'm glad you have returned to us."

"Returned from where?"

"For the past four days, you've been drifting in and out of consciousness." He reached down and patted the boy on his head. "I see you've met my grandson. He is named for me. Roberto Rawlins."

His grandson? Why was this doctor using Luke's last name. "What year is it?"

The young version of Roberto giggled. "2006. Everybody knows that."

Sixty years had passed since she'd been with Luke at Camp Hale. The world was an utterly different place.

This doctor in his seventies had to be the adult version of the ten-year-old orphan from

Italy. She looked into his eyes. "Luke came back to Italy for you."

"Yes. He saved my life."

That meant Luke had survived. He'd recovered from his wounds and returned to Italy to find Roberto. "Where is he? Where's Luke?"

"This might take some explanation." He leaned down and whispered something to the youthful Roberto who gave a nod, then darted from the room.

Dr. Roberto Rawlins sat on the bed beside her. Gently, he took her hand and felt for her pulse. "I've heard a lot about you, Shana Parisi. After Luke rescued me from Italy, we came to live here. In Aspen."

"We're in Aspen?"

He nodded. "As I'm sure you know, the ski industry in Aspen became a big business after World War II. Luke was a part of that development. He became a very wealthy man."

"I told him to invest in Aspen," she remembered.

"But wealth wasn't the reason he chose to live here. He wanted to be close to the place where he'd last been with you. There was no other woman for him. Not ever."

Tears welled up behind her eyelids. Luke had lived a life of unrequited love. "He never married?"

"He swore that he was engaged. To you."

She looked down at her left hand. She was still wearing Luke's 10th Mountain Division ring on the middle finger. Reaching up, she dashed the tears from her cheeks. She should have been with him, should have been a part of his life. Damn it, she was supposed to be married to him.

But Luke had survived and lived his life. He had to be in his nineties by now. But she didn't care. She wanted to see him, to share whatever time they had left. "Where is he?"

"You have brought him back to us."

Brought him back? What did that mean?

Her gaze turned toward the door to her hospital room, and she saw him. He looked a little older and leaner. The creases at the edge of his breathtaking blue eyes had deepened. He was maybe in his forties.

In a few quick strides, he came to her bedside and gathered her into his arms. For a long moment, she held him. When his lips joined with hers, her heart began to beat again. The shredded fabric of her life knitted back together into a full, beautiful tapestry. She had found her destiny.

"I missed you," he murmured. "Every day, I missed being with you."

"Is this really happening?" She nuzzled against the crook of his neck. "Are you really here?"

"It wasn't a dream, Shana."

She was vaguely aware that Roberto had left the room and closed the door. She and Luke were alone.

Much as she hated to be rational at this moment, she couldn't stop herself. "You have to explain this to me."

"Time travel." He chuckled. "I like this little turnaround. This time, I'm the one with the secrets."

If she hadn't been so overjoyed to see him, she would have been angry. "Tell me."

"I'm not sure how or why I traveled through time. After you disappeared from Camp Hale and I recovered, I talked to Dr. Fermi about you and time travel. He told me that some observable phenomenon can't be explained because scientific knowledge doesn't have the tools to comprehend."

"The Fermi paradox," she said.

"But I knew, by instinct, that we'd be together again. Every year on May sixth, I returned to the cabin and waited for the right conditions. The blizzard. The gusts of whirling snow and wind."

His devotion touched her heart. He'd been ready to throw himself into a time vortex to find her.

"Roberto was nineteen when it happened. He was already in college and on his way to becoming a doctor. Every year, before I left for the cabin, I made sure he'd be well cared for, and I told him that this was something I had to do. He understood."

When Roberto told her that she'd brought Luke back to them, this is what he meant. "You disappeared?"

"Apparently. The last thing I remember from fifty years ago is a glowing light and the blizzard. Then I looked up and saw you on the slopes, crashing downhill." He exhaled a long sigh. "It was beautiful, Shana."

"I doubt that." She remembered falling. Not a good thing.

"I scooped you up and brought you here to the hospital. You've been in and out of consciousness for the past four days."

"I'm here now." She felt herself smiling all over. "And I'll never leave you again."

When he linked his fingers through hers, she saw a gold ring on his pinkie finger. The shard of green trinite gleamed brilliantly.

"I love you," he said. "Will you marry me?"

"Ask that question a thousand times and my answer will always be the same. Yes."

"There's someone else here who wants to see you."

He rose from her bed and went to the door. Her father stood outside. In his expression, Shana saw his love for her and she finally understood that she wasn't a disappointment to him. He was proud of her.

"Sir," Luke said to him. "I want to ask your permission to marry your daughter."

Her father beamed. "As soon as possible."

All these men gathered around her. Dr. Roberto Rawlins and his grandson. Her father. And Luke.

She couldn't take her eyes off this incredible, handsome man who had come through time and overcome all the odds to be with her again.

In the back of her mind, she heard her mother's voice as she gave her fairy-tale blessing. "And they all lived happily ever after."

* * * * *

Run, Ally! Don't be fooled by him. He's evil. Don't let him touch you!

But as the forbidding figure came through the mists toward her, Ally knew she couldn't run. His features burned with dark malevolence, and his physical domination of everything around him seemed to hold her like a net.

She'd heard the tales. She knew all about the Wolverton legend and the ghost that haunted The Willows, an elegant old mansion lost by Micha Wolverton nearly a hundred years ago. According to folklore, the estate was stolen from the Wolvertons, and Micha was killed, trying to reclaim it. His dying vow was to be reunited with the spirit of his beloved wife, who'd taken her life for reasons no one would speak of, except in whispers. But Ally had never put much stock in the fantasy. She didn't believe in ghosts.

Until now—

She still didn't understand what was happening. The figure had materialized out of the mist that lay thick on the damp cemetery soil. A cool breeze and silvery moonlight had played against the ancient stone of the crypts surrounding her, until they joined the mist, causing his body to thicken and solidify right before her eyes. That was when she realized she'd seen this man before. Or thought she had, at least.

His face was familiar...so familiar, yet she couldn't put it together. Not with him looming so near. She stepped back as he approached.

"Don't be afraid," he said. His voice wasn't what she expected. It didn't sound as if it were coming from beyond the grave. It was deep and sensual. Commanding.

"Who are you?" she managed.

"You should know. You summoned me."

"No, I didn't." She had no idea what he

was talking about. Two minutes ago, she'd been crouching behind a moss-covered crypt, spying on the mansion that had once been The Willows, but was now Club Casablanca. And then this—

If he was Micha, he might be angry that she was trespassing on his property. "I'll go," she said. "I won't come back. I promise."

"You're not going anywhere."

Words snagged in her throat. "Wh-why not? What do you want?"

"If I wanted something, Ally, I'd take it. This is about need."

His words resonated as he moved within inches of her. She tried to back away, but her feet were useless. "And you need something from me?"

"Good guess." His tone burned with irony. "I need lips, soft and surrendered, a body limp with desire."

"My lips, my bod—?"

"Only yours."

"Why? Why me?" This couldn't be Micha. He didn't want any woman but Rose. He'd died trying to get back to her.

"Because you want that, too," he said.

Wanted what? A ghost of her own? She'd always found the legend impossibly romantic, but how could he have known that? How could he know anything about her? Besides, she'd sworn off inappropriate men, and what could be more inappropriate than a ghost? She shook her head again, still not willing to admit the truth. But her heart wouldn't play along. It clattered inside her chest. The mere thought of his kiss, his touch, terrified her. This wildness, it was fear, wasn't it?

When his fingertips touched her cheek, she flinched, expecting his flesh to be cold, lifeless. It was anything but that. His skin was smooth and hot, gentle, yet demanding. And while his dark brown eyes were filled with mystery and wonder, there was a sensitivity about them that threatened to disarm her if she looked too deeply.

"These lips are mine," he said, as if stating a universal fact that she was helpless to avoid. In truth, it was just that. She couldn't stop him.

And she didn't want to.

* * * * *

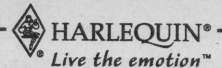

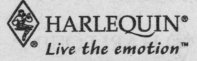

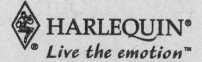

HARLEQUIN®

Super Romance®

...there's more to the story!

Superromance.
A *big* satisfying read about unforgettable characters. Each month we offer *six* very different stories that range from family drama to adventure and mystery, from highly emotional stories to romantic comedies—and much more! Stories about people you'll believe in and care about. Stories too compelling to put down....

Our authors are among today's *best* romance writers. You'll find familiar names and talented newcomers. Many of them are award winners—and you'll see why!

If you want the biggest and best in romance fiction, you'll get it from Superromance!

Exciting, Emotional, Unexpected...

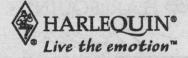

HARLEQUIN®
Live the emotion™

HARLEQUIN®
Presents

**The world's bestselling romance series...
The series that brings you your favorite authors,
month after month:**

Helen Bianchin...Emma Darcy
Lynne Graham...Penny Jordan
Miranda Lee...Sandra Marton
Anne Mather...Carole Mortimer
Susan Napier...Michelle Reid

and many more uniquely talented authors!

Wealthy, powerful, gorgeous men...
Women who have feelings just like your own...
The stories you love, set in exotic, glamorous locations...

HARLEQUIN®
Presents

Seduction and Passion Guaranteed!

HPDIR104